Eight superb s.f. tales, including . . .

A story about a spaceman in a life hutch on an airless planetoid who is held prisoner by a deranged robot . . .

Another about a galactic agent who learns that there is a cosmic reason for his distasteful, dangerous job . . .

One about a robot guarding a treasure, who plays a tricky question-and-answer game with those who come seeking it . . .

And the classic story about the strangest space trip of all – to Far Centaurus . . .

Also by Robert Silverberg

SUNDANCE AND OTHER SCIENCE FICTION STORIES
MUTANTS (edited by Silverberg)

and published by Corgi Books

EDITED BY
Robert Silverberg

Deep Space

CORGI BOOKS
A DIVISION OF TRANSWORLD PUBLISHERS LTD

DEEP SPACE
A CORGI BOOK o 552 10551 1

Originally published in Great Britain by
Abelard Schumann Limited

PRINTING HISTORY
Abelard Schumann edition published 1976
Corgi edition published 1977

This book is set in 10pt Imprint

Corgi Books are published by Transworld Publishers Ltd.,
Century House, 61–63 Uxbridge Road,
Ealing, London, W.5.
Made and printed in Great Britain by
Hunt Barnard Printing Ltd., Aylesbury, Bucks.

Contents

Acknowledgments

'Blood's a Rover,' by Chad Oliver. Copyright © 1952 by Street & Smith Publications, Inc. Reprinted by permission of the author.

'Noise,' by Jack Vance. Copyright © 1952 by Better Publications, Inc. Reprinted by permission of the author and his agents, Scott Meredith Literary Agency, Inc., 580 Fifth Avenue, New York, N.Y. 10036.

'Life Hutch,' by Harlan Ellison. Copyright © 1956 by Quinn Publishing Co., Inc. Reprinted by permission of the author and his agent, Robert P. Mills, Ltd.

'Ticket to Anywhere,' by Damon Knight. Copyright © 1952 by Galaxy Publishing Corporation. Reprinted by permission of the author and his agent, Robert P. Mills, Ltd.

'The Sixth Palace,' by Robert Silverberg. Copyright © 1965 by Galaxy Publishing Corporation. Reprinted by permission of the author and his agents, Scott Meredith Literary Agency, Inc.

'Lulungomeena,' by Gordon R. Dickson. Copyright © 1953 by Galaxy Publishing Corporation. Reprinted by permission of the author and his agent, Robert P. Mills, Ltd.

'The Dance of the Changer and the Three,' by Terry Carr. Copyright © 1968 by Joseph Elder. Reprinted by permission of the author.

'Far Centaurus,' by A. E. van Vogt. Copyright © 1944 by Street & Smith Publications, Inc. Reprinted by permission of the author and his agent, Forrest J. Ackerman.

Introduction

Reality keeps making life complicated for the writers of science fiction. Every day we move into the future at a remorseless rate, and as the present becomes the past, huge areas of what once had been the domain of science fiction are conquered. No longer can one write of the first manned voyages to the moon or the first probes of Mars and Venus or the first controlled nuclear reaction: those belong to history now, not to science fiction. Not only technological progress but the growth of scientific understanding deprive science-fictionists of their cherished themes. Because a good science-fiction writer plays according to the rules of science, he is no longer free to write of creatures native to the moon (as H. G. Wells did) or feudal principalities on Mars (as Edgar Rice Burroughs did) or unchanging hemispheres of darkness and light on Mercury (as practically everybody did). We have learned too much about those places, and as a result, certain tempting areas of speculation are denied to us by the inexorable hand of scientific truth. Science tells us that the other worlds and moons of our solar system are inhospitable, forbidding places; we are not likely to find intelligent civilizations on them, or even any very advanced life-forms at all. And this imposes restrictions on today's science-fiction writers that did not inhibit the tale spinners of previous generations.

But the universe is a big place. It still offers dizzying, limitless possibilities to the writer of science fiction who wishes to unleash his imagination and give it full play. He need only move out beyond the rim of the solar system, past the orbit of Pluto, into the uncharted vastnesses of deep space. There lie stars beyond counting, whole galaxies and clusters of galaxies, an infinite array of wonders and miracles. We know a good deal about the realm of deep space, but ever so much more is still a mystery to us, and where mystery exists, science fiction has room to explore. We can postulate planets of astonishing colors and textures and shapes, alien species of life, solar systems that dance in delicious intricacy around

9

multiple suns – anything at all, so long as it does not blatantly contradict the underlying laws of the universe as we think we understand them today. An inexhaustible treasure trove of virtually unbounded probability awaits those whose imaginations voyage to the stars. Here are eight such voyages, only a thin sample of the wonders that science-fiction writers have brought back from that uncharted and all-encompassing realm of infinity known as deep space.

—ROBERT SILVERBERG

Blood's a Rover

CHAD OLIVER

*Symmes C. Oliver is an anthropologist ; his special fields
of interest are the Plains Indians and the ethnology of
East Africa, and he holds the title of chairman of the
Department of Anthropology at the University of Texas
at Austin. Chad Oliver is a science-fiction writer whose
stories, usually based on anthropological themes, have won
him a wide and enthusiastic readership over the past
twenty-odd years. The two Olivers are, of course, the
same man : Chad Oliver's science-fiction stories draw
freely on Symmes C. Oliver's deep and rich background
in anthropology, and Professor Oliver approaches his
studies of primitive tribes with a science-fictionist's wide-
open receptiveness to strangeness. The benefits of such an
interchange are evident in this warm-hearted and moving
tale of distant worlds.*

> Clay lies still, but blood's a rover;
>   Breath's a ware that will not keep.
> Up, lad : when the journey's over
>   There'll be time enough to sleep.
> —*A. E. Housman.*

I

Night sifted through the city like flakes of soft black
snow drifting down from the stars. It whispered along the
tree-lined canyons between the clean shafts of white buildings
and pressed darkly against windows filled with warm light.
Conan Lang watched the illumination in his office increase
subtly in adjusting to the growing darkness outside and then
looked again at the directive in his hand.

It still read the same way.

'Another day, another world,' he said aloud. And then,
paraphrasing: 'The worlds are too much with us—'

Conan Lang fired up his pipe and puffed carefully on it to

get it going properly. Then he concentrated on blowing neat cloudy smoke rings that wobbled across the room and impaled themselves on the nose of the three-dimensional portrait of the President. It wasn't that he had anything against President Austin, he assured himself. It was simply that Austin represented that nebulous being, Authority, and at the moment it happened that Authority was singularly unwelcome in the office of Conan Lang.

He looked back at the directive. The wording was friendly and informal enough, but the meaning was clear:

Headquarters, Gal. Administration.
Office of Admiral Nelson White,
Commander, Process Planning Division.
15 April, 2701. Confidential.

One Agent Conan Lang
Applied Process Corps
G. A. Department Seven
Conan:

We got another directive from the Buzzard yesterday. Seems that the powers that be have decided that a change in Sirius Ten is in order – a shift from Four to Five. You're it. Make a prelim check and report to me at your convenience. Cheer up – maybe you'll get another bag of medals out of it.

Nelson.

Conan Lang left the directive on his desk and got to his feet. He walked over to the window and looked out at the lights sprinkled over the city. There weren't many. Most people were long ago home in the country, sitting around the living room, playing with the kids. He puffed slowly on his pipe.

Another bag of medals. Nelson wasn't kidding anybody – wasn't even trying to, really. He knew how Conan felt because he felt the same way. They all did, sooner or later. It was fascinating at first, even fun, this tampering with the lives of other people. But the novelty wore off in a hurry – shriveled like flesh in acid under a million eyes of hate, a million talks with your soul at three in the morning, a million shattered lives. Sure, it was necessary. You could always tell yourself that; that was the charm, the magic word that was supposed to make everything fine and dandy. Necessary – but for *you*, not for them. Or perhaps for them too, in the long run.

Conan Lang returned to his desk and flipped on the intercom. 'I want out,' he said. 'The Administration Library,

Division of Extraterrestrial Anthropology. I'd like to speak to Bailey if he's there.'

He had to wait thirty seconds.

'Bailey here,' the intercom said.

'This is Lang. What've you got on Sirius Ten?'

'Just like that, huh? Hang on a second.'

There was a short silence. Conan Lang smoked his pipe slowly and smiled as he visualized Bailey punching enough buttons to control a space fleet.

'Let's see,' Bailey's voice came through the speaker. 'We've got a good bit. There's McAllister's "Kinship Systems of Sirius Ten"; Jenkins' – that's B. J. Jenkins, the one who worked with Holden – "Sirius Ten Social Organization"; Bartheim's "Economic Life of Sirius Ten"; Robert Patterson's "Basic Personality Types of the Sirius Group"; "Preliminary and Supplementary Ethnological Surveys of the Galactic Advance Fleet" – the works.'

Conan Lang sighed. 'O.K.,' he said. 'Shoot them out to my place, will you?'

'Check – be there before you are. One thing more, Cone.'

'Yes?'

'Been reading a splendid eight-volume historical novel of the Twentieth Century. Hot stuff, I'll tell you. You want me to send it along in case you run out of reading material?'

'Very funny. See you around.'

'So long.'

Conan Lang switched off the intercom and destroyed the directive. He tapped out his pipe in the waster and left the office, locking the door behind him. The empty hallway was sterile and impersonal. It seemed dead at night, somehow, and it was difficult to believe that living, breathing human beings walked through it all day long. It was like a tunnel to nowhere. He had the odd feeling that there was nothing around it at all, just space and less than space – no building, no air, no city. Just a white antiseptic tunnel to nowhere.

He shook off the feeling and caught the lift to the roof. The cool night air was crisp and clean and there was a whisper of a breeze out of the north. A half moon hung in the night, framed by stars. He looked up at it and wondered how Johnny was getting along up there, and whether perhaps Johnny was even then looking down on Earth.

Conan Lang climbed into his bullet and set the controls.

The little ship rose vertically on her copter blades for two thousand feet, hovered a moment over the silent city, and then flashed off on her jets into the west.

Conan Lang sat back in his cushioned seat, looking at the stars, trying not to think, letting the ship carry him home.

Conan Lang relaxed in his armchair, his eyes closed, an icy bourbon and soda in his hand. The books he had requested – neat, white, uniform microfilm blowups from the Administration Library – were stacked neatly on the floor by his side, waiting. Waiting, he thought, sipping his drink. They were always waiting. No matter how much a man knew, there was always more – waiting.

The room closed in around him. He could feel it – warm, friendly, personal. It was a good room. It was a room filled with life, his life and Kit's. It was almost as if he could see the room better with his eyes closed, for then he saw the past as well as the present. There was the silver and black tapestry on the wall, given to him by old Maharani so long ago, on a world so far away that the very light given off by its sun when he was there had yet to reach the Earth as the twinkle of a star in the night sky. There were his books, there were Kit's paintings, there was the smudge – the current one – on the carpet where Rob had tracked dirt into the house before supper.

He opened his eyes and looked at his wife.

'I must be getting old, Kit,' he said. 'Right at the moment, it all looks pretty pointless.'

Kit raised her eyebrows and said nothing.

'We tear around over the galaxy like a bunch of kids playing Spacemen and Pirates,' he said, downing his drink. 'Push here, pull there, shove here, reverse there. It's like some kind of half-wit game where one side doesn't even know it's playing, or on which side of the field. Sometimes – '

'Want another drink?' Kit asked softly.

'Yes. Kit – '

'I know,' she said, touching his shoulder with her hand. 'Go ahead and talk; you'll feel better. We go through this every time there's a new one, remember? I know you don't really mean things the way you say them, and I know why you say them that way anyhow.' She kissed him lightly on the forehead and her lips were cool and patient. 'I understand.'

Conan Lang watched her leave the room with his empty

glass. 'Yes,' he whispered to himself. 'Yes, I guess you do.'

It *was* necessary, of course. Terribly, urgently necessary. But it got to you sometimes. All those people out there, living their lives, laughing and crying, raising children. It hurt you to think about them. And it wasn't necessary for them, not for him, not for Kit. Or was it? You couldn't tell; there was always a chance. But if only they could just forget it all, just live, there was so much to enjoy –

Kit handed him a fresh bourbon and soda, icy and with just a trace of lemon in it the way he liked it, and then curled up again on the couch, smiling at him.

'I'm sorry, angel,' he said. 'You must get pretty sick of hearing the same sad song over and over again.'

'Not when you sing it, Cone.'

'It's just that sometimes I chuck my mind out the nearest window and wonder why – '

There was a thump and a bang from the rear of the house. Conan Lang tasted his drink. That meant Rob was home. He listened, waiting. There was the hollow crack – that was the bat going into the corner. There was the heavy thud – that was the fielder's glove.

'That's why,' Kit said.

Conan Lang nodded and picked up the first book off the floor.

Three days later, Conan Lang went up the white steps, presented his credentials, and walked into the Buzzard's Cage. The place made him nervous. Irritated with himself, he paused deliberately and lit his pipe before going on. The Cage seemed cold, inhuman. And the Buzzard –

He shouldn't feel that way, he told himself, again offering his identification before entering the lift to the Nest. Intellectually, he understood cybernetics; there was nothing supernatural about it. The Cage was just a machine, for all its powers, even if the Buzzard did sometimes seem more – or perhaps less – than a man. Still, the place gave him the creeps. A vast thinking machine, filling a huge building, a brain beside which his own was as nothing. Of course, men had built it. Men made guns, too, but the knowledge was scant comfort when you looked into a metallic muzzle and someone pulled the trigger.

'Lang,' he said to himself, 'you're headed for the giggle ward.'

He smiled then, knowing it wasn't so. Imagination was a prime requisite for his job, and he just had more than his share. It got in the way sometimes, but it was part of him and that was that.

Conan Lang waded through a battery of attendants and security personnel and finally reached the Nest. He opened the door and stepped into the small, dark room. There, behind the desk where he always was, perched the Buzzard.

'Hello, Dr Gottleib,' said Conan Lang.

The man behind the desk eyed him silently. His name was Fritz Gottleib, but he had been tagged the Buzzard long ago. No one used the name to his face, and it was impossible to tell whether or not the name amused him. He spoke but seldom, and his appearance, even after you got used to it, was startling. Fritz Gottleib was squat and completely bald. He always dressed in black and his heavy eyebrows were like horizontal splashes of ink against the whiteness of his face. The Buzzard analogy, thought Conan Lang, was more than understandable; it was inevitable. The man sat high in his tower, in his Nest of controls, brooding over a machine that perhaps he alone fully understood. Alone. He always seemed alone, no matter how many people surrounded him. His was a life apart, a life whose vital force pulsed in the shifting lights of the tubes of a great machine.

'Dr Lang,' he acknowledged, unmoving, his voice almost a croak.

Conan Lang puffed on his pipe and dropped into the chair across from Gottleib. He had dealt with the Buzzard before and most of the shock had worn off. You could get used to anything, he supposed. Man was a very adaptable animal.

'The smoke doesn't bother you, I hope?'

Gottleib did not comment. He simply stared at him, his dark eyes unblinking. Like looking at a piece of meat, thought Conan Lang.

'Well,' he said, trying again, 'I guess you know what I'm here for.'

'You waste words,' Fritz Gottleib hissed.

'I hadn't realized they were in short supply,' Lang replied, smiling. The Buzzard was irritating, but he could see the justice in the man's remark. It *was* curious the number of useless things that were said all the time – useless, at any rate, from a purely communicative point of view. It would have been sheerly incredible for Gottleib – who after all, had been checking his results in the computer – *not* to have known the nature of his mission.

'Okay,' said Lang, 'what's the verdict?'

Fritz Gottleib fingered a square card in his surprisingly long-fingered hands, seeming to hover over it like a bird of prey.

'It checks out,' he said sibilantly, his voice low and hard to hear. 'Your plan will achieve the desired transfer in Sirius Ten, and the transfer integrates positively with the Plan.'

'Anything else? Anything I should know?'

'We should all know many more things than we do, Dr Lang.'

'Um-m-m. But that was all the machine said with respect to my proposed plan of operations?'

'That was all.'

Conan Lang sat back, watching Gottleib. A strange man. But he commanded respect.

'I'd like to get hold of that baby sometime,' he said easily. 'I've got a question or two of my own.'

'Sometimes it is best not to know the answers to one's questions, Dr Lang.'

'No. But I'd like to have a shot at it all the same. Don't tell the security boys I said that; they'd string me up by the toes.'

'Perhaps one day, Dr Lang. When you are old like me.'

Conan Lang stood up, cupping his pipe in his hand. 'I guess that's all,' he said.

'Yes,' said Fritz Gottleib.

'See you around.'

No answer. Cold shadows seemed to fill the room.

Conan Lang turned and left the way he had come. Behind him, drilling into his back, he could feel the eyes of Fritz Gottleib following him, cold and deep like the frozen waters of an arctic sea.

The ship stood on Earth but she was not of Earth. She was poised, a mighty lance of silver, a creature of the deeps. She waited, impatient, while Conan Lang slowly walked across the vast duralloy tarmac of Space One, Admiral White at his side. The sun was bright in a clean blue sky. It touched the ship with lambent flame and warmed Conan Lang's shoulders under his uniform. A slight puff of breeze rustled across the spaceport, pushing along a stray scrap of white paper ahead of it.

'Here we go again,' said Conan Lang.

'That's what you get for being good,' the admiral said with a smile. 'You get good enough and you'll get my job – which ought to be a grim enough prospect even for you. If you're smart, you'll botch this job six ways from Sunday, and then we'll have to give you a rest.'

'Yeah – play a little joke, strictly for laughs, and give 'em an atom bomb or two to stick on the ends of their hatches. Or take 'em back to the caves. There are plenty of delicious possibilities.'

The two men walked on, toward the silver ship.

'Everything's set, I suppose?' asked Conan Lang.

'Yep. Your staff is already on board and the stuff is loaded.'

'Any further instructions?'

'No – you know your business, or you wouldn't be going. Just try to make it as quick as you can, Cone. They're getting warm over on Research on that integration-acceleration principle for correlating data – it's going to be big, and I'll want you around when it breaks.'

Conan Lang grinned. 'What happens if I just up and disappear one day, Nels? Does the galaxy moan and lie down and quit?'

'Search me,' said Admiral Nelson White. 'But don't take any more risks than you absolutely have to. Don't get the idea that you're indispensable, either. It's just that it's tiresome to break in new men.'

'I'll try to stay alive if you're positive that's what you want.'

They approached the ship. Kit and Rob were waiting. The admiral touched his cap and moved on, leaving Conan Lang alone with his family. Kit was lovely – she always was, Conan Lang thought. He couldn't imagine a life without her.

'Bye, darlin',' he whispered, taking her in his arms. 'One of these days I'm coming back and I'm never going to leave you again.'

'This is till then,' Kit said softly and kissed him for keeps.

Much later, Conan Lang released her and shook hands with his son.

'So long, old-timer,' he said.

'Hurry back, Dad,' Rob said, trying not to cry.

Conan Lang turned and joined Admiral White at the star cruiser. He did not look back.

'Good luck, Cone,' the admiral said, patting him on the back. 'I'll keep the medals warm and a light in the cabin window.'

'Okay, Nels,' said Conan Lang.

He swung aboard the great ship and stepped into the lift. There was a muted hum of machinery as the car whispered up through the pneumatic tube, up into the hollowness of the ship. Already it seemed to Conan Lang that he had left Earth far behind him. The endless loneliness of the star trails rode up with him in the humming lift.

The ship rested, quiescent, on Earth. Ahead of her, calling to her, the stars flamed coldly in an infinite sea of night.

II

Conan Lang walked down the long white corridor to the after-hold, his footsteps muffled and almost inaudible in the murmur of the atomics. It *would* be a long white corridor, he thought to himself. Wherever man went, there went the long white corridors – offices, hospitals, command posts. It was almost as if he had spent half a lifetime walking through long white corridors, and now here was yet another one – cold and antiseptic, hanging in space eight light-years from Earth.

'Halt.'

'Lang here,' he told the Fleetman. 'Kindly point that thing the other way.'

'Identification, please.'

Lang sighed and handed it over. The man should know him by now; after all, the ship was on his mission, and he was hardly a subversive character. Still, orders were orders – a principle that covered a multitude of sins. And they couldn't afford to take chances, not *any* chances.

'All right, sir,' the Fleetman said, returning the identification. 'Sorry to bother you.'

'Forget it,' said Conan Lang. 'Keep your eye peeled for space pirates.'

The guard smiled. 'Who'd want to steal space, sir?' he asked. 'It's free, and I reckon there's enough to go around.'

'Your inning,' acknowledged Conan Lang, moving into the afterhold. The kid was already there.

'Hello, sir,' said Andrew Irvin.

'Hi, Andy – and cut the "sir", what do you say? You make me feel like I should be extinct or embalmed or something.'

The kid smiled almost shyly. Conan Lang had half expected to find him there in the hold; Andy was always poking around, asking questions, trying to learn. His quick brown eyes and alert carriage reminded Conan of a young hunting dog, frisking through the brush, perpetually on the verge of flushing the grandfather of all jackrabbits.

'It doesn't seem possible, does it?' asked the kid.

Conan Lang raised his eyebrows.

'All this, I mean,' Andy Irvin said, gesturing at the neat brown sacks stacked row upon row in the brightly lighted hold. 'To think that a couple of sacks of that stuff can remold a planet, change the lives of millions of people – '

'It's not just the sacks, Andy. It took man a good many hundreds of thousands of years to learn what to *do* with those sacks.'

'Yes, sir,' the kid said, hanging on every word.

'No "sir," remember? I'm not giving you a lecture, and you don't have to look attentive. I'm sure that elementary anthropology isn't *too* dumbfounding to a guy who took honors at the Academy.'

'Well – '

'Never mind.' Conan Lang eyed him speculatively. The kid reminded him, almost too much, of someone else – a kid named Conan Lang who had started out on a great adventure himself too many years ago. 'I . . . um-m-m . . . guess you know you're going to work with me on Ten.'

Andy looked like Conan had just handed him a harem on a silver platter. 'No, sir,' he said. 'I didn't know. Thank you, sir.'

'The name is Conan.'

'Yes, sir.'

'Hellfire,' said Conan Lang. How did you go about telling a kid that you were happy to have someone around with stars in his eyes again? Without sounding like a fool? The answer was simple – you didn't.

'I can't wait,' Andy said. 'To really *do* something at last – it's a great feeling. I hope I'll do okay.'

'It won't be long now, Andy. Twenty-four hours from now

you and I go to work. The buggy ride is about over.'

The two men fell silent then, looking at the neat brown rows of sacks, feeling the star ship tremble slightly under them with the thunder of her great atomics.

It was night on Sirius Ten – a hot, humid night with a single moon hanging like frozen fire in the darkness. A small patrol craft from the cruiser floated motionless in the night sky, her batteries pouring down a protective screen around the newly cleared field. Conan Lang wiped the sweat from his forehead and washed his hands off in the clean river water that gurgled through the trench at his feet.

'That about does it, Andy,' he said wearily. 'Toss 'em a Four signal.'

Andy Irvin turned the rheostat on his small control board to Four and flipped the switch. They waited, listening to the faint murmur of the night breeze off the river. There was no change, nothing that they could see, but they could almost feel the intense radiation pounding into the field from the patrol ship, seeping into the ground, accelerating by thousands of times the growth factor in the seeds.

'That's got it,' said Conan Lang. 'Give 'em release.'

Andy shot the patrol craft the release signal and shut off his control board. The little ship seemed to hover uncertainly. There was a humming sound and a spot of intense white light in the sky. That was all. The ship was gone and they were alone.

'It's been a long night, kid,' yawned Conan Lang. 'We'd better get some sack time – we're liable to need it before morning.'

'You go ahead,' Andy Irvin said. 'I'm not sleepy; the sunrise here ought to be something.'

'Yeah,' said Conan Lang. 'The sunrise ought to be something.'

He walked across the field and entered a structure that closely resembled a native hut in appearance but was actually quite, quite different. Too tired even to undress, he piled into bed with his clothes on and rested quietly in the darkness.

The strange, haunting, familiar-with-a-difference sounds of an alien world whispered around the hut on the soft, moist breeze from the sluggish river. Faraway, an animal screamed hoarsely in the clogging brush. Conan Lang kept his eyes closed and tried not to think, but his mind ignored him. It went right on working, asking questions, demanding answers, bringing up into the light many memories that were good and some that were better forgotten.

'Kit,' he said, very softly.

Tired as he was, he knew there would be no sleep for him that night.

The sunrise was a glory. The blue-white inferno of Sirius hung in the treetops across the field and then climbed into the morning sky, her white dwarf companion a smaller sun by her side. The low cumulus clouds were edged with flame – fiery red, pale blue, cool green. The fresh morning winds washed the field with air, and already the young plants were out of the ground, thirsty for the sun. The chuckling water in the trenches sparkled in the light.

With the morning, the natives came.

'They're all around us,' Conan Lang said quietly.

'I can't see them,' whispered Andy Irvin, looking at the brush.

'They're there.'

'Do you . . . expect trouble, sir?'

'Not yet, assuming we've got this deal figured right. They're more afraid of us than we are of them.'

'What if we *don't* have it figured right?'

Conan Lang smiled. 'Three guesses,' he said.

The kid managed a wry grin. He was taking it well, Lang thought. He remembered how he'd felt the first time. It didn't really hit you until that first day, and then it upped and kicked you in the teeth. Quite suddenly, it was all a very different proposition from the manuals and the viewers and the classrooms of the Academy. *Just you, all alone*, the alien breeze sighed in your ear. *You're all alone in the middle of nowhere*, the wind whispered through the trees. *Our eyes are watching you, our world is pressing you back, waiting. What do you know of us really? What good is your knowledge now?*

'What next?' Andy asked.

'Just tend the field, kid. And try to act like a ghost. You're an ancestor of those people watching us from the brush, remember. If we've got this figured wrong – if those survey reports were haywire somewhere, or if someone's been through here who didn't belong – you should have a little warning at least. They don't use blowguns or anything – just spears, and they'd prefer a hatchet. If there's trouble, you hightail it back to the hut *at once* and man the projector. That's all.'

'I'm not so sure I care to be an ancestor,' Andy Irvin muttered, picking up his hoe. 'Not yet, anyhow.' He moved off along a water trench, checking on the plants.

Conan Lang picked up his own hoe and set to work. He could feel the natives watching him, wondering, whispering to themselves. But he was careful not to look around him. He kept his head down and dug at the plants with his hoe, clearing the water channels. The plants were growing with astonishing rapidity, thanks to the dose of radiation. They should be mature in a week. And then –

The sun blazed down on his treated skin and the sweat rolled off his body in tiny rivulets. The field was strangely silent around him; there was only the gurgle of the water and the soft sigh of the humid breeze. His hoe chopped and slushed at the mud and his back was tired from bending over so long. It was too still, unnaturally still.

Behind that brush, back in the trees – a thousand eyes.

He did not look around. Step by step, he moved down the trench, under the hellish sun, working with his hoe.

The fire-burned days and the still, hushed nights alternated rapidly. On the morning of the third day, Andy Irvin found what they had been waiting for.

In the far corner of the field, placed on a rude wood platform about four feet high, there were three objects. There was a five-foot-square bark mat, neatly woven. There was a small animal that closely resembled a terrestrial pig, face down, its throat neatly slashed. And there was a child. It was a female baby, evidently not over a week old. It had been strangled to death.

'It's . . . different . . . when you see it for yourself,' Andy said quietly, visibly shaken.

'You'll get used to it,' said Conan Lang, his voice purposely flat and matter-of-fact. 'Get the pig and the mat – and stop looking like a prohibitionist who just found a jug of joy water in the freezer. This is old stuff to ancestors.'

'Old stuff,' repeated Andy without conviction.

They carried the contents of the platform back to their hut

and Conan Lang wrapped the body of the child in a cloth.

'We'll bury her tonight after dark,' he said. 'The pig we eat. It won't do any harm to sit on the mat where they can see us while we're eating it, either.'

'Well,' Andy muttered. 'Glad to see you're not going to eat the baby, too.'

'You never can tell,' smiled Conan Lang. 'We anthropologists are all crazy, or hadn't you heard?'

'I've heard,' agreed Andy Irvin, getting his nerves under control again. 'Where's the hot sauce?'

Conan Lang stepped back outside and picked up his hoe. The blazing double sun had already produced shimmering heat waves that danced like live things in the still air over the green field. The kid was going to be all right. He'd known it all along, of course – but you could never be *sure* of a man until you worked with him under field conditions. And a misfit, an unstable personality, was anything but a joke on an alien planet where unknowable forces hung in the balance.

'Let's see if I've got this thing figured straight,' Andy said, puffing away on one of Conan's pipes. 'The natives are afraid of us, and still they feel that they must make us an offering because we, as their supposed ancestors, control their lives. So they pick a system of dumb barter rather than sending out the usual contact man to ferret out kinship connections.'

'You're okay so far,' Conan Lang said. 'I guess you've studied about the dumb barter systems used on Earth in the old days; it was used whenever trade took place between groups of markedly unequal strength, such as the African pygmies and trading vessels from the west. There's a fear factor involved.'

'Yes, sir.'

'Forget the "sir". I didn't mean to lecture. I think I'll start calling you Junior.'

'Sorry. The bark mat is a unit in a reciprocal trade system and the pig is a sacred animal – I get that part of it. But the baby – that's terrible, Conan. After all, we caused that death in a way –'

'Afraid not,' Conan Lang corrected him. 'These people practice infanticide; it's part of their religion. If the preliminary reports were correct – and they've checked out so far – they kill all the female children born on the last three days of alternate months. There's an economic reason, too – not enough food to go around, and that's a pretty effective method of birth control. The baby would have been killed regardless – we had nothing to do with it.'

'Still – '

'I know. But maybe she was the lucky one after all.'

'I don't quite follow you there.'

'Skip it – you'll find out soon enough.'

'What are you going to leave them tonight?'

'Not sure yet,' Conan Lang said. 'We'll have to integrate with their value system, of course. We brought some mats, and I guess a good steel knife won't hurt things any. We'll worry about that later. Come on, farmer – back to work.'

Andy Irvin picked up his hoe and followed Conan Lang into the field. The clear water bubbled softly as it flowed through the trenches. The growing plants sent their roots thirstily into the ground and the fresh green shoots stretched up like tentacles into the humid air of Sirius Ten.

That night, under the great yellow moon that swam faraway and lonesome among the stars, they placed exchange gifts of their own on the platform. Next morning, the invisible traders had replaced them with four mats and another dead pig.

'No babies, anyhow,' Andy Irvin said, puffing industriously on one of Conan's pipes. They had decided that cigarettes, as an unfamiliar cultural trait to the natives, were out. Now, with Andy taking with unholy enthusiasm to pipe smoking, Conan Lang was threatened with a shortage of tobacco. He watched the smoke from the kid's pipe with something less than ecstasy.

'We can have smoked ham,' he observed.

'It was your idea,' Andy grinned.

'Call me "sir".'

Andy laughed, relaxed now, and picked up the pig. Conan gathered up the somewhat cumbersome mats and followed him back into the hut. The hot, close sun was already burning his shoulders. The plants were green and healthy looking, and the air was a trifle fresher in the growing field.

'Now what?' Andy asked, standing outside the hut and letting the faint breeze cool him off as best it could.

'I figure we're about ready for an overt contact,' Conan Lang said. 'Everything has checked out beautifully so far, and the natives don't seem to be suspicious or hostile. We might as well get the ball rolling.'

'The green branch, isn't it?'

'That's right.'

They still did not get a glimpse of the natives throughout the steaming day, and that night they placed a single mat on the platform. On top of the mat they put a slim branch of green leaves, twisted around back on itself and tied loosely to form a circle. The green branch was by no means a universal symbol of peace, but, in this particular form, it chanced to be so on Sirius Ten. Conan Lang smiled a little. Man had found many curious things among the stars, and most of them were of just this unsensational but very useful sort.

By dawn, the mat and the circle branch were gone and the natives had left them nothing in return.

'Today's the day,' Conan Lang said, rubbing the sleep out of his eyes. 'They'll either give us the works or accept our offer. Nothing to do now but wait.'

They picked up their hoes and went back into the field. Waiting can be the most difficult of all things, and the long, hot morning passed without incident. The two men ate their lunch in silence, thankful for the odorless injection that kept the swarming insects away from them. Late in the afternoon, when the long blue shadows of evening were already touching the green plants and the clean, flowing water, the natives came.

There were five of them and they appeared to be unarmed. One man walked slightly in advance of the others, a circular branch of green leaves in his hand. Conan Lang waited for them, with Andy standing by at his side. It was moments like this, he thought, that made you suddenly realize that you were all alone and a long, long way from friends. The natives came on steadily. Conan felt a surge of admiration for the young man who led them. From his point of view, he was walking into a situation filled with the terror of the supernatural, which was a very real part of his life. His steps did not falter. He would, Conan supposed, be the eldest son of the most powerful chief.

The natives stopped when they were three paces away. Their leader extended the circular green branch. 'We would serve you, fathers from the mountains,' the native said in his own tongue.

Conan Lang stepped forward and received the branch. 'We

are brothers,' he replied in the same language, 'and we would be your friends.'

The native smiled, his teeth very white. 'I am Ren,' he said. 'I am your brother.'

Conan Lang kept his face expressionless, but deep within him a dark regret and sadness coursed like ice through his veins.

It had begun again.

III

For many days, Conan Lang listened to the Oripesh natives preparing for the feast. Their small village, only a quarter of a mile from the field, was alive with excitement. The women prepared great piles of the staple ricefruit and broiled river fish in great green leaves on hot coals. The men chanted and danced interminably, cleansing the village by ritual for the coming visitation, while the children, forgotten for once, played on the banks of the river. On the appointed day, Conan Lang walked into the village with Andy Irvin at his side.

It was a crude village, necessarily so because of its transient nature. But it was not dirty. The natives watched the two men with awe, but they did not seem unfriendly. The supernatural was for them always just on the other side of the hill, hidden in the night, and now it was among them, in the open. That was all. And what, after all, thought Conan Lang, could have seemed more supernatural to them than a silver ship that dropped out of the stars? What was supernatural depended on one's point of view – and on how much one happened to know about what was *natural*.

The box he carried was heavy, and it took both arms to handle it. He watched Andy puffing at his side and smiled.

'Stick with it, kid,' he said, walking steadily through the watching natives. 'You may earn your pay yet.'

Andy muttered something under his breath and blinked to get the sweat out of his eyes.

When they reached the clearing in the center of the village, they stopped and put their boxes down. Ren, the eldest son of the chief Ra Renne, approached them at once and offered them a drink from a large wooden bowl. Conan drank and passed the container on to Andy, who grinned broadly and took a long swallow of the warm fluid. It was sweet, although

27

not too sweet, and it burned pleasantly on the way down. It was, Conan decided instantly, a great improvement over some native fermented horrors he had been subjected to in times past.

The natives gathered around them in a great circle. There must have been nearly five hundred of them – far more than the small village could accommodate for any length of time.

'We're celebrities,' Conan Lang whispered out of the side of his mouth as he waited to be presented ceremonially to the chiefs.

'You want my autograph?' asked Andy, his face just a trifle flushed from the drink he had taken. 'I make a real fine X.'

The feast followed a pattern familiar to Conan Lang. They were presented ceremonially to the tribe, having identified themselves as ancestors of four generations ago, thus making themselves kin to virtually all the tribe with their complicated lineage system, and also making refutation impossible since no one remembered that far back. They were seated with the chiefs, and ate the ritual feast rapidly. The food was good, and Conan Lang was interested in getting a good taste of the rice-fruit plant, which was the basic food staple of the Oripesh.

After the eating came the drinking, and after the drinking the dancing. The Oripesh were not a musical people, and they had no drums. The men and the women danced apart from each other, each one doing an individual dance – which he owned, just as the men from Earth owned material property – to his own rhythm pattern. Conan Lang and Andy Irvin contented themselves with watching, not trusting themselves to improvise an authentic dance. They were aware that their conduct was at variance with the somewhat impulsive conduct usually attributed to ancestors in native folklore, but that was a chance they had to take. Conan was very conscious of one old chief who watched him closely with narrowed eyes.

Conan ignored him, enjoying the dancers. The Oripesh seemed to be a happy people, although short on material wealth. Conan Lang almost envied them as they danced – envied them for their simple lives and envied them their ability to enjoy it, an ability that civilized man had left by the wayside in his climb up the ladder. Climb – or descent? Conan Lang sometimes wondered.

Ren came over, his color high with the excitement of the

dance. Great fires were burning now, and Conan noticed with surprise that it was night.

'That is Loe,' he said, pointing. 'My *am-ren*, my bride-to-be.' His voice was filled with pride.

Conan Lang followed his gesture and saw the girl. Her name was a native word roughly translatable as *fawn*, and she was well named. Loe was a slim, very shy girl of really striking beauty. She danced with diffidence, looking into Ren's eyes. The two were obviously, almost painfully, in love – love being a part of the culture of the Oripesh. It was difficult to realize, sometimes, even after years of personal experience, that there were whole worlds of basically humanoid peoples where the very concept of romantic love did not exist. Conan Lang smiled. Loe was, if anything, a trifle *too* beautiful for his taste. Dancing there, with the yellow moon in her hair, moving gracefully with the leaping shadows from the crackling fires, she was ethereal, a fantasy, like a painting of a woman from another, unattainable century.

'We would give gifts to the chiefs,' Conan Lang said finally. 'Your Loe – she is very beautiful.'

Ren smiled, quickly grateful, and summoned the chiefs. Conan Lang rose to greet them, signaling to Andy to break open the boxes. The chiefs watched intently. Conan Lang did not speak. He waited until Andy had opened both boxes and then pointed to them.

'They are yours, my brothers,' he said.

The natives pressed forward. A chief picked the first object out of the box and stared at it in disbelief. The shadows flickered eerily and the night wind sighed through the village. He held the object up to the light and there was a gasp of astonishment.

The object was a ricefruit – a ricefruit the likes of which had never before been seen on Sirius Ten. It was round, fully a foot in diameter, and of a lush, ripe consistency. It made the potato-sized ricefruits of the Oripesh seem puny by comparison.

It was then that Conan Lang exploded his bombshell.

'We have come back to show you, our brothers, how to grow the great ricefruit,' he said. 'You can grow them over and over again, *in the same field*. You will never have to move your village again.'

The natives stared at him in wonder, moving back a little in fear.

'It cannot be done,' a chief whispered. 'The ricefruit devours the land – every year we must move or perish.'

'That is over now,' Conan Lang said. 'We have come to show you the way.'

The dancing had stopped. The natives waited, nervous, suddenly uncertain. The yellow moon watched through the trees. As though someone had flipped a switch, sound disappeared. There was silence. The great ricefruit was magic. They looked at the two men as though seeing them for the first time. This was not the way of the past, not the way of the ancestors. This was something completely *new*, and they found themselves lost, without precedent for action. Ren alone smiled at them, and even he had fear in his eyes.

Conan Lang waited tensely. He must make no move; this was the crisis point. Andy stood at his side, very still, hardly breathing.

A native walked solemnly into the silence, carrying a young pig under his arm. Conan Lang watched him narrowly. The man was obviously a shaman, a witch doctor, and his trembling body and too-bright eyes were all too clear an indication of why he had been chosen for his role in the society.

With a swiftness of motion that was numbing, the shaman slit the pig's throat with a stone knife. At once he cut the body open. The blood stained his body with crimson. His long, thin hands poked into the entrails. He looked up, his eyes wild.

'They are not ancestors,' he screamed, his voice high like a hysterical woman's. 'They have come to do us evil!'

The very air was taut with tension.

'No,' Conan Lang said loudly, keeping his voice clear and confident. 'The *barath-tui*, the shaman, has been bewitched by sorcerers! Take care that you do not offend your ancestors!'

Conan Lang stood very still, fighting to keep the alarm off his face. He and Andy were helpless here, and he knew it. They were without weapons of any sort – the native loincloth being a poor place to conceal firearms. There was nothing they could do – they had miscalculated, moved too swiftly, and now they were paying the price.

'We are your brothers,' he said into the ominous silence. 'We are your fathers and your father's fathers. There are others who watch.'

The flames leaped and danced in the stillness. An old man

stepped forward. It was the chief that Conan had noticed watching him before.

'You say you are our brothers who have taken the long journey,' the old chief said. 'That is good. We would see you walk through the fire.'

The wind sighed in the trees. Without a moment's hesitation, Conan Lang turned and walked swiftly toward the flames that crackled and hissed in the great stone fire pits.

There was nothing else in all the world except the flickering tongues of orange flame that licked nearer and nearer to his face. He saw the red, pulsing coals waiting beneath the twisted black branches in the fire and he closed his eyes. The heat singed his eyebrows and he could feel his hair shrivel and start to burn.

Conan Lang kept moving, and moved fast. He twisted a rigid clamp on his mind and refused to feel pain. He wrenched his mind out of his body, thinking as he had been trained to think, until it was as if his mind floated a thing apart, free in the air, looking down upon the body of Conan Lang walking through hell.

He knew that one of the attributes of the Oripesh ancestor gods was that they could walk through flame without injury – a fairly common myth pattern. He had known it before he left Earth. He should have been prepared, he knew that. But man was not perfect, which would have been a dangerous flaw had it not been his most valuable characteristic.

He saw that his legs were black and blistered and he smelled the suffocating smell of burning flesh. The smoke was in his head, in his lungs, everywhere, choking him. Some of the pain was coming through –

He was out. He felt Andy's hands beating out the rivulets of flame that clung to his body and he forced the clean, pure air of night into his sick lungs. The pain, the pain –

'Stick with it, Cone,' Andy whispered in his ear. 'Stick with it.'

Conan Lang managed to open his eyes and stared blankly into a hot-red haze. The haze cleared, and he was faintly surprised to find that he could still see. The natives were awestruck with fear – they had angered their gods, and death was in the air. Conan Lang knew that the shaman who had denounced him would quite probably be dead of fear before the night was over – if he did not die before then of some less subtle malady. He had endangered the tribe without reason, and he would pay with his life.

Conan Lang kept his face expressionless. Inside, he was on fire. Water, he had to have water, cold water –.

Ren came to him, his eyes filled with pain. 'I am sorry, my brother,' he whispered. 'For my people, I am sorry.'

'It is all right, Ren,' Conan Lang heard his voice say steadily. 'I am, of course, unharmed.'

Conan Lang touched Andy's arm and moved across to the chiefs. He felt Andy standing behind him, ready to catch him, just in case. He could feel nothing in his feet – quite suddenly, he was convinced that he was standing on the charred stumps of his legs and he fought to keep from looking down to make sure he still had feet.

'You have doubted your brothers who have come far to help their people,' he said quietly, looking directly into the eyes of the old chief who had sent him into the flames. 'We are disappointed in our people – there are sorcerers at work among you, and they must be destroyed. We leave you now. If you anger your brothers again, the Oripesh shall cease to be.'

He did not wait for an answer but turned and started away from the clearing, back through the village. Andy was at his side. Conan Lang set his teeth and moved at a steady pace. He must have no help until they were beyond the village; the natives must not suspect –

He walked on. The great yellow moon was high in the night sky, and there was the face of Loe with stars in her hair. The moon shuddered and burst into flame, and he heard himself laughing. He bit his lips until the blood came and kept going, into the darkness, into nothing. The pain clawed at his body.

They were through the village. Something snapped in Conan Lang – the steel clamp that had carried him through the nightmare parted with a clean *ping*. There was emptiness, space. Conan Lang collapsed. He felt Andy's arm around him, holding him up.

'You'll have to carry me, kid,' he whispered. 'I can't walk at all.'

Andy Irvin picked him up in his arms and set out through the night.

'It should have been me,' he said in bitter self-reproach. 'It should have been me.'

Conan Lang closed his eyes, and at last nothing mattered any more, and there was only darkness.

A week later, Conan Lang stood in the dawn of Sirius Ten, watching the great double sun lift above the horizon and chase the shadows from the green field that they had carved out of the wilderness. He was still a very sick man, but Andy had pulled him through as best he could, and now the star cruiser was coming in to pick him up and leave a replacement with the kid.

The fresh leaves of the ricefruit plants were shoulder high, and the water in the irrigation trenches chuckled cleanly, waiting for the full fury of the sun. The tenuous, almost hesitant breeze crawled through the still air.

Conan Lang watched the green plants silently. The words of the dead *barath-tui*, the shaman, echoed in his brain. *They are not ancestors*, the man had screamed. *They have come to do us evil!*

They have come to do us evil. . . .

How could he have known – with only a pig and a stone knife? A crazy shaman working the discredited magic of divination – and he had been *right*. Coincidence? Yes, of course. There was no other way to look at it, no other *sane* way. Conan Lang smiled weakly. He remembered reading about the Snake Dance of the Hopi, long ago back on Earth. The Snake Dance had been a rain-making ceremonial, and invariably when the very early anthropologists had attended the dance they had got drenched on the way home. It was only coincidence and good timing, of course, but it was difficult to tell yourself that when the rain began to pour.

'Here she comes,' said Andy Irvin.

There was a splitting whistle and then a soft hum as a small patrol ship settled down toward the field on her anti-gravs. She hung there in the dawn like a little silver fish seen through the glassite walls of a great aquarium, and Conan Lang could sense what he could not see – the massive bulk of the sleek star cruiser waiting out in space.

The patrol ship came down out of the sky and hovered a few feet off the ground. A man swung down out of the outlift and waved. Conan Lang recognized him as Julio Medina, who had been lifted out of another sector of Sirius Ten to come in and replace him with Andy. The ricefruit was green and fresh

3

in the field, and it hurt Conan to leave his job unfinished. There wasn't a great deal to do now until the check, of course, and Julio was a very competent and experienced man, but there was still so much that could go wrong, so much that you could never anticipate –

And he didn't want anything to happen to the kid.

'So long, Cone,' Andy said, his voice very quiet. 'And – thanks. I won't forget what you did.'

Conan Lang leaned on Andy's arm and moved toward the ship. 'I'll be back, Andy,' he said, trying to keep the weight off his feet. 'Hold the fort – I know it'll be in good hands.'

Conan Lang shook hands with Julio and then Julio and Andy helped him into the outlift. He had time for a brief wave and a final glimpse of the green field under the fiery sun, and then he was inside the patrol ship. They had somehow rigged up a bunk for him in the cramped quarters, and he collapsed into it gratefully.

'Home, James,' he whispered, trying not to think about what would happen if they could not save his legs.

Conan Lang closed his eyes and lay very still, feeling the ship pulse and surge as it carried him out into the dark sea from which he had come.

IV

The doctors saved his legs, but years were to pass before Conan Lang again set foot upon Earth. Space was vast and star cruisers comparatively few. In addition, star ships were fabulously expensive to operate – it was out of the question for a ship on a mission to make the long run from Sirius to Sol for the sake of one man. Conan Lang became the prize patient of the ship medics, and he stayed with the star cruiser as it operated in the Sirius area.

A star cruiser on operations was never dull, and there were books to read and reports to write. Conan Lang curbed his impatience and made the best of the situation. The local treatments applied by Andy had been effective enough so that the ship medics were able to regenerate his burned tissue, and it was only a question of time before he would be strong again.

The star cruiser worked efficiently and effectively in support of Administration units in the Sirius area, sliding through the blackness of space like some leviathan of the deep, and Conan Lang rested and made himself as useful as he could. He often went up into the control room and stood watching the visiplate that looked out upon the great emptiness of space. Somewhere, on a far shore of that mighty sea, was a tiny planet called Earth. There, the air was cool and fresh under the pines, and the beauty of the world, once you got away from it and could see it in perspective, was fantastic. There were Rob and Kit, friendship and tears and laughter.

There was home.

While his body healed, Conan Lang lived on the star cruiser. There was plenty of time to think. Even for a race with a life span of almost two hundred years, the days and the weeks and the months can seem interminable. He asked himself all the old questions, examined all the old answers. Here he was, on a star ship light-years from home, his body burned, waiting to go back to Sirius Ten to change the life of a planet. What thin shreds of chance, what strange webs of history, had put him there? When you added up the life of Conan Lang, of all the Conan Langs, what did you get? Where was Earth going, that pebble that hurled its puny challenge at the infinite?

Sometimes, it was all hard to believe.

It had all started, he supposed, with cybernetics. Of course, cybernetics itself was but the logical outgrowth of a long cultural and technological trend. For centuries, man's ally, the machine, had helped him physically in his adjustment to his environment. What more natural than that it should one day help him mentally as well? There was really nothing sinister about thinking machines, except to a certain breed of perpetually gloomy poets who were unable to realize that values were never destroyed but were simply molded into new patterns in the evolution of culture. No, thinking machines were fine and comforting – for a while.

But with the dawn of space travel, man's comfortable, complacent progress toward a vague somewhere was suddenly knocked into a cocked hat. Man's horizons exploded to the rims of the universe with the perfection of the star drive – he was no longer living *on* a world but *in* an inhabited universe. His bickerings and absurdities and wars were seen as the petty things they were – and man in a few tremendous years emerged at last from adolescence.

Science gave to men a life span of nearly two hundred active years and gave him the key to forever. But there was a catch, a fearful catch. Man, who had had all he could do to survive the conflicts of local groups of his own species, was suddenly faced with the staggering prospect of living in an inhabited *universe*. He had known, of course, about the millions and millions of stars, about the infinity of planets, about the distant galaxies that swam like island universes through the dark seas of space. But he had known about them as figures on a page, as photographs, as dots of unwinking light in a telescope. They had been curiosities, a stimulus to the imagination. Now they were vital parts of his life, factors to be reckoned with in the struggle for existence. In the universe were incredible numbers of integers to be equated in the problem of survival – *and the mind of man could not even learn them all, much less form intelligent conclusions about future actions*.

And so, inevitably, man turned again to the machine. But this time there was a difference. The machine was the only instrument capable of handling the data – and man in a million years could not even check its most elementary conclusions. Man fed in the facts, the machine reached the conclusions, and man acted upon them – not through choice, but simply because he had no other guide he could trust.

Men operated the machines – but the machines operated men.

The science of cybernetics expanded by leaps and bounds. Men made machines to develop new machines. The great mechanical brains grew so complex that only a few men could even pretend to understand them. Looking at them, it was virtually impossible to believe that they had been born in the minds of men.

The machines did not interfere in the everyday routine of living – man would never submit to that, and in problems which he could understand he was still the best judge of his own happiness. It was in the larger problems, the problems of man's destiny in the universe in which he found himself, that the great brains were beyond value. For the machines could integrate trends, patterns, and complexes of the known worlds and go on from there to extrapolate into the unknown. The machines could, in very general terms, predict the outcome of any given set of circumstances. They could, in a very real sense, see into the future. They could see where Earth was headed.

And Earth was headed for disaster.

The machines were infallible. They dealt not with short-term probabilities, but with long-range certainties. And they stated flatly that, given the equation of the known universe, Earth would be destroyed in a matter of centuries. There was only one thing to do – man must change the equation.

It was difficult for man, so recently Earthbound, to really *think* and *act* in terms of an inhabited universe. But the machines showed conclusively that in as yet inaccessible galaxies life had evolved that was physically and mentally hostile to that of Earth. A collision of the two life-forms would come about within a thousand years, and a life-and-death struggle was inevitable. The facts were all too plain – Earth would lose and the human race would be exterminated.

Unless the equation could be changed.

It was a question of preparing the galaxy for combat. The struggle would be a long one, and factors of reserves, replacements, different cultural approaches to common problems, planets in varying stages of development, would be important. It was like a cosmic chess game, with worlds aligning themselves on a monstrous board. In battles of galactic dimensions, the outcome would be determined by centuries of preparation before contact was even made; it was not a romantic question of heroic spaceships and iron-jawed men of action, but rather one of the cultural, psychological, technological, and individual patterns which each side could bring to bear – patterns which were the outgrowths of millennia of slow evolution and development.

Earth was ready, or would be by the time contact came. But the rest of the galaxy – or at any rate as much of it as they had managed to explore – was not, and would not be. The human race was found somewhere on most of the star systems within the galaxy, but not one of them was as far advanced as were the men from Earth. That was why Earth had never been contacted from space – indeed, it was the only possible explanation, at least in retrospect. And the other galaxies, with their totally alien and forever nonunderstandable principles, were not interested in undeveloped cultures.

The problem thus became one of accelerating the cultural

evolution of Earth's sister planets by means of diffusion, in order to build them up into an effective totality to combat the coming challenge. And it had to be done in such a manner that the natives of the planets were completely unaware that they were not the masters of their own destiny, since such a concept produced cultural stagnation and introduced corrupting elements into the planetary configurations. It had often been argued that Earth herself was in such a position, being controlled by the machines, but such was not the case – their choice had been a rational one, and they could abandon the machines at any time at their own risk.

Or so, at any rate, argued the thinkers of Earth.

The long months lengthened into years, and, inactive though he was, Conan Lang spent his time well. It was good to have a chance to relax and think things through; it was good for the soul to stop midway in life and take stock. Almost, it was possible to make sense out of things, and the frantic rush to nowhere lost some of its shrieking senselessness.

Conan Lang smiled without humor. That was all very well for him, but what about the natives whose lives they were uprooting? Of course, they were human beings, too, and stood to lose as much as anyone in the long run – but they did not understand the problem, *could* not understand it. The plain truth was that they were being used – used for their own benefit as well as that of others, but used nonetheless.

It was true that primitive life was no bed of roses – it was not as if, Conan Lang assured himself, the men from Earth were slithering, serpentlike, into an idyllic Garden of Eden. All they were doing was to accelerate the normal rate of change for a given planet. But this caused far-reaching changes in the culture as it existed – it threw some people to the dogs and elevated others to commanding positions. This was perhaps no more than was done by life itself, and possibly with better reason, but you couldn't tell yourself that when you had to face the eyes of a man who had gone from ruler to slave because of what you had done.

The real difficulty was that you couldn't *see* the threat. It was there all right – a menace beside which all the conflicts of the human race were as nothing. But it had always been difficult for men to work before the last possible moment, to prepare rather than just sit back and hope for the best. That man was working now as he had never worked before, in the face of an unseen threat from out of the stars, even to save his own existence, was a monument to his hard-won maturity. It would have been so easy, so pleasant, just to take it easy and enjoy a safe and comfortable life – and beyond question it would have meant the end of the human race.

Of one thing, Conan Lang was sure – whenever man stopped trying, stopped working and dreaming and reaching for impossible heights, whenever he settled back in complacency, on that day he shrank to atrophied insignificance.

Sirius Ten had been a relatively easy project because of the planet-wide nature of its culture. Sirius Ten had only one huge land mass, and one great sea. The natives all shared basically the same life pattern, built around the cultivation of dry ricefruit, and the teams of the Applied Process Corps were faced with only one major problem rather than hundreds of them as was more often the case. It was true that certain peoples who lived on the shores of the sea, together with one island group, had a variant culture based on fishing, but these were insignificant numerically and could for practical purposes be ignored.

The dry ricefruit was grown by a cutting and burning method, under which a field gave a good yield only once before the land was exhausted and the people had to move on. Under these conditions, individual ownership of land never developed, and there were no inequalities of wealth to speak of. The joint families worked different fields every year, and since there was no market for a surplus there was no effort made to cultivate more land than was really needed.

The Oripesh natives of Sirius Ten had a well-developed cult of ancestor worship, thinking of their dead as always watching over them and guiding their steps. Since whatever the ancestors did automatically had the sanction of tradition behind it, it was through them that the Corps had decided to work – it being simply a question of palming off Corps agents as ancestors come back from their dwelling place in the mountains to help their people. With careful preparations and experienced men, this had not proved overly difficult – but there were always miscalculations, accidents. Men were not like chemicals, and they did not always react as they were supposed to react. There was always an individual variable to be considered. That was why if a Corps Agent lived long enough to retire you knew both that he knew his stuff and that he had had more than his share of plain old-fashioned luck.

Sirius Ten had to be shifted from Stage Four to Stage Five. This was a staggering change in economics, social structure, and technology - one that had taken men on Earth many centuries to accomplish. The men of the Applied Process Corps had to do it in a matter of a few years. And so they set out, armed with a variety of ricefruit that grew well in marshy land and a sound knowledge of irrigation.

With such a lever they could move a world.

It was three years to the day when Conan Lang returned to Sirius Ten. The patrol ship came in on her anti-gravs, and he waited eagerly for the outlift shaft to open. His heart was pounding in his chest and his lips were dry - it was almost like coming home again.

He swung his newly strong body into the outlift and came out of it in the green field he had planted so long ago. He took a deep breath of the familiar humid air and grinned broadly at the hot, burning sun over his head. It *was* good to be back - back at a place like so many other places he had known, places that were as close to a home as any he could ever have without Kit. The breeze whispered softly through the green ricefruit, and he waved at Julio, who came running across the field to meet him. These were, he knew, his kind of people - and he had missed Andy all these years.

'Hey there, Julio!' he laughed, shaking Medina's hand. 'How goes it?'

'Pretty good, Conan,' Julio said quietly. 'Pretty good.'

'The kid - how's the kid?'

'Andy is dead,' said Julio Medina.

Conan Lang stood stock-still while an iron fist smacked into his stomach with cold, monotonous precision. Andy dead. It could not be, *could not be*. There had been no word, nothing. He clenched his fists. It couldn't be true.

But it was. He knew that with ice-cold certainty.

'It just happened the other day, Conan,' Julio said. 'He was a fine boy.'

Conan Lang couldn't speak. *The whole planet*, his mind

tortured him. *The whole stinking planet isn't worth Andy's life.*

'It was an accident,' Julio said, his voice carefully matter-of-fact. 'Warfare has sprung up between the rival villages like we figured. Andy was out after information and he got between them – he was hit by mistake with a spear. He never had a chance, but he managed to walk away and get back here before he died. The Oripesh don't suspect that he wasn't a god and could die just like anyone else. He saved the rest of us by coming back here – that's something.'

'Yeah,' Conan Lang said bitterly, 'that's something.'

'I buried him here in the field,' Julio Medina went on. 'I thought he'd like that. He . . . said good-bye to you, Conan.'

It had been a long time since Conan Lang had had tears in his eyes. He turned without a word and walked away, across the green field and into the hut where he could be alone.

V

From that time on, by unspoken mutual consent, the two men never again mentioned the kid's name. They gave him the best possible write-up in their reports, and that was all that they could ever do for Andy Irvin.

'I think we've about done it here, Conan,' Julio told him. 'I'd like to have you make your own check and see if you come up with the same stuff I did. There's a lull in the raiding right now – the natives are worried because that spear hit an ancestor by mistake, and they're pretty well occupied with rituals designed to make us feel better about the whole thing. You shouldn't have any trouble, and that about ought to wind things up.'

Conan Lang nodded. 'It'll be good to get home again, eh, Julio?'

'Yes, you know that – and for you it should be for keeps.'

Conan Lang raised his eyebrows.

'It's no secret that you're due to be kicked upstairs,' Julio said. 'I rather think this is your last field job.'

'Well, it's a nice theory anyhow.'

'You remember all us old men out here in the stars, the slave labor of the Process Corps. Bring us all home, Conan, and we'll sit around in the shade and drink cold wine and fish and tell lies to each other.'

'Consider it done,' said Conan Lang. 'And I'll give you all some more medals.'

'I've got medals.'

'Can't have too many medals, Julio. They're good for what ails you.'

'They're not good for what ails *me*,' said Julio Medina.

Conan Lang smiled and fired up his pipe. *The kid*, his mind whispered. *The kid liked that pipe.* He thrust the thought from his mind. A man had to take death in his stride out here, he told himself. Even when it was a kid who reminded you of yourself a million years ago –

A million years ago.

'I'll start in tomorrow,' Conan Lang said, puffing on his pipe. 'Do you know Ren, Julio?'

'The chief's son? Yes.'

'How did he come out?'

'Not well, Conan. He lost his woman, Loe, to one of the men we made wealthy; he has not been the same since.'

'We're great people, Julio.'

'Yes.'

Conan Lang was silent then, and the two men stood together in the warm evening air, watching the great double sun float slowly down below the horizon as the long black shadows came marching up from the far edge of the world.

Next morning, Conan Lang was off with the dawn on his final check. He pretty well knew what he would find – Julio Medina was an experienced hand, and his information was reliable. But it was always a shock when you saw it for yourself. You never got used to it. To think that such a tiny, seemingly insignificant thing could change a planet beyond recognition. A ricefruit –

It was already hot when he passed the native fields. Their ricefruit plants were tall and healthy, and their irrigation channels well constructed. He shook his head and walked on to the native village.

Where the open, crude, friendly village had stood there was a great log wall. In front of the wall was a series of deep and ugly-looking moats. Behind the wall, he could see the tops of sturdy wooden buildings, a far cry from the huts of only a few short years ago. Conan Lang made no attempt at concealment but walked openly up to the moats and crossed

42

them on a log bridge. He stopped outside the closed gate.

'You will remember me who walked through the flames,' he said loudly in the Oripesh tongue. 'You will open the gate for your brother as he would visit you.'

For a moment nothing happened, and then the gate swung open. Conan Lang entered the village.

The native guard eyed him with suspicion, but he kept his distance. Conan Lang noticed that he had a bow by the log wall. There was nothing like constant warfare for the production of new weapons, he reflected. Civilization was bringing its blessings to the Oripesh with leaps and bounds.

Conan Lang walked through the village unmolested, taking rapid mental notes. He saw storehouses for ricefruit and observed slaves being marched off to work in the fields. The houses in the village were strong and comfortable, but there was a tense air in the village, a feeling of strain. Conan Lang approached a native and stopped him.

'Brother,' he said, 'I would see your chiefs. Where are they?'

The native looked at him warily. 'The Oripesh have no chiefs,' he said. 'Our king is in council.'

Conan Lang nodded, a sick feeling inside him. 'It is well,' he said. 'Ren – I would see him.'

The native jerked his thumb contemptuously toward the back of the village. 'He is there,' he said. 'Outside.'

Conan Lang moved through the village, watching, missing nothing. He went all the way through and came out through the back wall. There, the old-style native huts baked in squalor under the blazing sun. There was no log wall around them, although they were inside the moat system. A pig rooted around for garbage between the huts.

'Slums,' Conan Lang said to himself.

He walked among the huts, ignoring the fearful, suspicious eyes of the natives. He found Ren preparing to go out into the fields. The chief's son was thin. He looked tired, and his eyes were dull. He saw Conan and said nothing.

'Hello, Ren,' said Conan Lang.

The native just looked at him.

Conan Lang tried to think of something to say. He knew what had happened – the chiefs and their sons had been so busy with ritual work for the tribe that they had lagged behind in the cultivation of the new ricefruit. They had stuck to the old ways too long, and their people had passed them by.

43

'I can help you, my brother,' Conan Lang said softly. 'It is not too late.'

Ren said nothing.

'I will help you with a field of your own,' said Conan Lang. 'Will you let me help you?'

The native looked at him, and there was naked hate in his eyes. 'You said you were my friend,' he said. Without another word, he turned and left. He did not look back.

Conan Lang wiped the sweat from his forehead and went on with his work. The sensitive part of his mind retreated back into a dark, insulated corner, and he let his training take over. He moved along, asking questions, watching, taking mental notes.

A little thing, he thought.

A new kind of plant.

A week later, Conan Lang had completed his check. He sat by the evening cook fire with Julio, smoking his pipe, watching the shadows in the field.

'Well, we did a good job,' he said. 'It's awful.'

'It would have come without us,' Julio reminded him. 'It does no good to brood about it. It is tough, sometimes, but it is a small price to pay for survival.'

'Yes,' said Conan Lang. 'Sure.'

'Your results check out with mine?'

'Mostly. It's the same old story, Julio.'

Conan Lang puffed slowly on his pipe, reconstructing what had happened. The new ricefruit had made it valuable for a family to hang on to one piece of land that could be used over and over again. But only a limited amount of the land could be used, because of natural factors like the presence or absence of available water. The families that had not taken the plunge right away were virtually excluded, and the society was divided into the landed and the landless. The landless gradually had to move further and further from the main village to find land upon which to grow the older type of ricefruit – sometimes their fields were so far away that they could not make the round trip in a single day. And they could not get too far away and start over, because of the tribal warfare that had broken out between villages now that valuable stores of ricefruit were there for the taking. The old joint family cooperation broke down, and slaves became economically feasible.

Now that the village need not be periodically moved, it too became valuable and so was strongly fortified for defense. One old chief, grown powerful with fields of the staple rice-fruit, set himself up as a king, and the other chiefs went to work in his fields.

Of course, Sirius Ten was still in transition. While the old patterns were being destroyed, new ones, less obvious to the untrained eye, were taking their place. Disintegration and reintegration marched hand in hand, but it would be tough on the natives for a while. Process Corps techniques had speeded up the action almost beyond belief, but from here on in the Oripesh were on their own. They would go on and on in their individual development – although no two peoples ever went through exactly the same stages at the same time, it was possible to predict a general planet-wide trend. The Oripesh would one day learn to write, since they already had a crude pictographic system for ritual use. When the contact finally came from the hostile stars in the future, what histories would they have written? Who would they remember, what would they forget? Would there be any twisted legend or myth left that recalled the long-ago time when the gods had come out of the mountains to change the lives of their people?

That was the way to look at it. Conan Lang tapped out his pipe on a rock. Just look at it like a problem, a textbook example. Forget about the people, the individuals you could not help, the lives you had made and the lives you had destroyed. Turn off that part of your mind and think in terms of the long-range good.

Or try to.

'We're all through here, Julio,' Conan Lang said. 'We can head for home now.'

'Yes,' said Julio Medina. 'It has been a long time.'

The two men sat silently in the darkness, each thinking his own thoughts, watching the yellow moon sail through silver stars.

After the patrol ship had been signaled, there was nothing to do but wait until their pickup could be co-ordinated with the time schedules of the other Corps men and the operational schedule of the star cruiser. Conan Lang busied himself with his reports while Julio sprawled in the shade and devised intricate and impossible card games with a battered deck that was old enough to be in itself of anthropological interest.

Conan Lang was playing a game, too. He played it with his mind and he was a somewhat unwilling participant. His mind had played the game before, and he was tired of it, but there was nothing he could do about it. There wasn't any button that would turn his mind off, and while it was on, it played games.

It was engaged in putting two and two together.

This was not in itself uncommon, although it was not as widespread as some people fondly imagined it to be. But Conan Lang played the game where others did not see even one, much less a set of twos with a relationship between them. There is nothing so hard to see as what is termed obvious after the fact. Conan Lang's mind had played with the obvious all his life; it would not let well enough alone. He didn't like it, there were times when he would have preferred to junk it all and go fishing without a thought in his head, but he was stuck with it. When his mind wanted to play the game, it played and that was that.

While he waited for the patrol ship, his mind was playing with a set of factors. There was the history of Earth, taken as a vast overall sequence. There were thinking machines, atomic power, and the field techniques of the Process Corps. There was the fact that Earth had no record of ever having been contacted by another world – they had always done the contacting themselves. There was the new principle that Admiral White had spoken to him about, the integration-acceleration factor for correlating data. There was the incredible, explosive energy of man that had hurled him light-years into space. There was his defiant heart that could tackle the prodigious job of reshaping a galaxy when the chips were down.

Conan Lang put two and two together, and he did not get four. He got five.

He didn't know the answers yet, but he knew enough to formulate the right questions. From past experience, he knew that that was the toughest part of the game. Incorrect answers were usually the products of off-center questions. Once you had the right question, the rest was a matter of time.

The patrol ship came for them finally, and Conan Lang and Julio Medina walked across the soil of Sirius Ten for the last time. They crossed the field where the green plants grew, and neither tried to say what was in his heart. Three had come and only two could leave. Andy Irvin had lived and worked and dreamed only to fall on an alien planet light-years away from Earth that could have been his. He was part of the price that was exacted for survival – and he was also a kid with stars in his eyes who had gotten a rotten, senseless break.

After the patrol ship had gone, the green leaves of the rice-fruit plants stretched hungrily up toward the flaming sun. The clean water chuckled along the irrigation trenches, feeding the roots in the field. Softly, as though sad with all the memories it carried, the lonesome breeze whispered through the empty hut that had housed the men from Earth.

VI

Through the trackless depths of interstellar space the star cruiser rode on the power from her atomics. The hum that filled the ship was a good sound, and she seemed to quiver with pride and impatience. It did make a difference which way you were going in space, and the ship was going home.

Conan Lang paced through the long white corridors and walked around the afterhold where the brown sacks of rice-fruit had been. He read in the library and joked with the medics who had salvaged his burned body. And always ahead of him, swimming in the great emptiness of space, were the faces of Kit and of his son, waiting for him, calling him home again.

Rob must have grown a lot, he thought. Soon, he wouldn't be a boy any longer – he would be a man, taking his place in the world. Conan remembered his son's voice from a thousand quiet talks in the cool air of evening, his quick, eager eyes –

Like Andy's.

'*Dad, when I grow up can I be like you? Can I be an Agent and ride on the ships to other worlds and have a uniform and everything?*'

What could you tell your son now that you had lived so long and were supposed to know so much? That life in the Process Corps filled a man with things that were perhaps better unknown? That the star trails were cold and lonely? That there were easier, more comfortable lives? All that was true; all the

47

men who rode the ships knew it. But they knew, too, that for them this was the only life worth living.

The time passed slowly. Conan Lang was impatient to see his family again, anxious to get home. But his mind gave him no rest. There were things he had to know, things he *would* know before he went home to stay.

Conan Lang had the right questions now. He had the right questions, and he knew where the answers were hidden.

Fritz Gottleib.

The star cruiser had hardly touched Earth again at Space One before Conan Lang was outside on the duralloy tarmac. Since the movements of the star ships were at all times top-secret matters, there was no one at the port to greet him, and for once Conan was glad to have a few extra hours to himself. Admiral White wouldn't expect him to check in until tomorrow anyway, and before he saw Kit he wanted to get things straight once and for all.

The friendly sun of Earth warmed him gently as he hurried across the tarmac, and the air felt cool and fresh. He helped himself to an official bullet, rose into the blue sky, and jetted eastward over the city. His brain was seething, and he felt cold sweat in the palms of his hands. What was it that Gottleib had said to him on that long-ago day?

'*Sometimes it is best not to know the answers to one's questions, Dr Lang.*'

Well, he was going to know the answers anyhow. All of them. He landed the bullet in the space adjoining the cybernetics building and hurried inside, flashing his identification as he went. He stopped at a switchboard and showed his priority credentials.

'Call the Nest, please,' he told the operator. 'Tell Dr Gottleib that Conan Lang is down here and would like to see him.'

The operator nodded and spoke into the intercom. There was a moment's delay, and then he took his earphones off and smiled at Conan Lang.

'Go right on up, Dr Lang,' the operator said. 'Dr Gottleib is expecting you.'

Conan Lang controlled his astonishment and went up the lift and down the long white corridors. *Expecting* him? But that was impossible. No one even knew the star cruiser was coming back, much less that he was coming here to the Nest. Impossible –

All around him in the great building he felt the gigantic mechanical brain with its millions of circuits and flashing tubes. The brain crowded him, pressed him down until he felt tiny and insignificant. It hummed and buzzed through the great shielded walls.

Laughing at him.

Conan Lang pushed past the attendants and security men and opened the door of the Nest. He moved into the small, dark room and paused to allow his eyes to become accustomed to the dim light. The room was silent. Gradually, the shadow behind the desk took form and he found himself looking into the arctic eyes of Fritz Gottleib.

'Dr Lang,' he croaked softly. 'Welcome to the Buzzard's Nest.'

The man had not changed; he was timeless, eternal. He was still dressed in black, and it might have been minutes ago instead of years when Conan Lang had last seen him. His black eyebrows slashed across his white face, and his long-fingered hands were bent slightly like claws upon his desk.

'How did you know I was coming here?' Now that he was face to face with Gottleib, Conan Lang felt suddenly uncertain, unsure of himself.

'I know many things, Dr Lang,' Fritz Gottleib said sibilantly. 'Had I cared to, I could have told you ten years ago the exact date, within a day or so, upon which we would have this meeting. I could even have told you what you would say when you came through the door, and what you are going to say five minutes from now.'

Conan Lang just stared at him, feeling like an absurd little child who had presumed to wrestle a gorilla. His mind recoiled from the strange man before him, and he knew at last that he knew nothing.

'I do not waste words, Dr Lang,' Gottleib said, his eyes cold and unmoving in his head. 'You will remember that when we last met you said you wanted to ask some questions of the machine. Do you remember what I said, Dr Lang?'

Conan Lang thought back across the years. *'Perhaps one day, Dr Lang,'* Gottleib had said. *'When you are old like me.'*

'Yes,' said Conan Lang. 'Yes, I remember.'

'You were not ready then,' Dr Gottleib said, his white face ghostly in the dim light. 'You could not even have framed the right questions, at least not all of them.'

Conan Lang was silent. How much *did* Gottleib know? Was there anything he *didn't* know?

'You are old enough now,' said Fritz Gottleib.

He turned a switch, and the surface of his desk glowed with dull red light. His face, reflected in the flamelike glow, was unearthly. His cold eyes looked out of hell. He rose to his feet, seeming to loom larger than life, filling the room. Moving without a sound, he left the room, and the door clicked shut behind him.

Conan Lang was alone in the red room. His heart hammered in his throat and his lips were dry. He clenched his fists and swallowed hard. Alone –

Alone with the great machine.

Conan Lang steadied himself. Purposefully, he made himself go through the prosaic, regular motions of lighting up his pipe. The tobacco was healthily full-bodied and fragrant, and it helped to relax him. He smoked slowly, taking his time.

The red glow from the desk filled the room with the color of unreality. Crimson shadows seemed to crouch in the corners with an impossible life of their own. But was anything impossible, here? Conan Lang felt the pulse of the great machine around him and wondered.

Trying to shake off a persistent feeling of dreamlike unreality, Conan Lang moved around and sat down behind Gottleib's desk. The red panel was a maze of switches which were used to integrate it with technical panels in other sections of the building. In the center of the panel was a keyboard on an open circuit to the machine and set into the desk was a clear square like a very fine telescreen. Conan Lang noticed that there was nothing on Gottleib's desk that was not directly connected with the machine – no curios, no pictures, no paperweights, not a single one of the many odds and ends most men picked up for their desks during a long lifetime. The whole room was frightening in its very impersonality, as though every human emotion had been beaten out of it long ago and the room had been insulated against its return.

The machines never slept, and the circuits were open. Conan Lang had only to ask, and any question that could be answered would be answered. The red glow in the room reminded him of the fire, and he shuddered a little in spite of himself. Had that really been over three years ago? How much had he learned in those three years when he had seen the Oripesh change before his eyes and had had time for once to really think his life through? How much did he still have to learn?

Conan Lang took a long pull on his pipe and set the desk panel for manual-type questioning and visual-screen reception. He hesitated a moment, almost afraid of the machine at his disposal. He didn't *want* to know, he suddenly realized. It wasn't like that. It was rather that he *had* to know.

Framing his words carefully, Conan Lang typed out the question that had been haunting him for years:

Is the earth itself the subject of process manipulation?

He waited nervously, sure of the answer but fearful of it nevertheless. There was a faint, all but inaudible hum from the machine and Conan Lang could almost feel the circuits closing in the great walls around him. The air was filled with tension. There was a brief click, and one word etched itself blackly on the clear screen:

Yes.

Conan Lang leaned forward, sure of himself now, and typed out another question.

How long has the Earth been manipulated, and has this control been for good or evil?

The machine hummed and answered at once.

The Earth has been guided since earth year nineteen hundred a.d. The second part of your question is meaningless.

Conan Lang hesitated, staggered in spite of himself by the information he was getting. Then he typed rapidly:

With reference to good, equate survival of the human race.

The screen clouded, cleared, and the words formed.

The control has been for good.

Conan Lang's breathing was shallow now. He typed tensely:

Has this control come from within this galaxy? if so, where? is there usually an agent other than Earth's in charge of this machine?

The hum of the machine filled the blood-red room, and the screen framed the answers.

THE CONTROL HAS COME FROM WITHIN THE GALAXY. THE SOURCE IS A WORLD KNOWN AS RERMA, CIRCLING A STAR ON THE EDGE OF THE GALAXY WHICH IS UNKNOWN TO EARTH. THE MAN KNOWN AS GOTTLEIB IS A RERMAN AGENT.

Conan Lang's pipe had been forgotten and gone out. He put it down and licked his dry lips. So far so good. But the one prime, all-important question had not yet been asked. He asked it.

IF THE PLAN IS FOLLOWED, WHAT WILL BE THE FINAL OUTCOME WITH RESPECT TO RERMA AND THE EARTH?

The machine hummed again in the red glow, and the answer came swiftly, with a glorious, mute tragedy untold between its naked lines:

RERMA WILL BE DESTROYED. THE EARTH WILL SURVIVE IF THE PLAN IS CAREFULLY FOLLOWED.

Conan Lang felt tears in his eyes, and he was unashamed. With time forgotten now, he leaned forward, asking questions, reading replies, as the terrible, wonderful story unfolded.

Far out on the edge of the galaxy, the ancient planet of Rerma circled her yellow sun. Life had evolved early on Rerma – had evolved early and developed fast. While the other humanoid peoples of the galaxy were living in caves, the Rerma were building a great civilization. When Earth forged its first metal sword, the Rerma split the atom.

Rerma was a world of science – true science. Science had eliminated war and turned the planet into a paradise. Literature and the arts flourished hand in hand with scientific progress, and scientists worked surrounded by cool gardens in which graceful fountains splashed and chuckled in the sun. Every man was free to develop himself as an individual, and no man bent his head to any other man.

The Rerma were the human race in full flower.

But the Rerma were few, and they were not a warlike people. It was not that they would not fight in an emergency, but simply that they could not possibly win an extended encounter. Their minds didn't work that way. The Rerma had evolved to a point where they were too specialized, too well adjusted to their environment.

And their environment changed.

It was only a question of time until the Rerma asked the right questions of their thinking machines and came up with the knowledge that their world, situated on the edge of the galaxy, was directly in the path of a coming cultural collision between two star systems. The Rerma fed in the data over and over again, and each time the great machines came up with the same answer.

Rerma would be destroyed.

It was too late for the equation to be changed with respect to Rerma – she had gone too far and was unfortunately located. But for the rest of the human race, scattered on the far-flung worlds that marched along the star trails, there was a chance. There was time for the equation to be changed for them – if only someone could be found to change it! For the Rerma had the knowledge, but they had neither the manpower nor the driving, defiant spirit to do the job themselves. They were capable of making heroic decisions and sticking by them, but the task of remolding a star system was not for them. That was a job for a young race, a proud and unconquerable race. That was a job for the men of Earth.

The ships of the Rerma found Earth in the earth year 1900. They knew that in order for their plan to succeed the Rerma must stand and fight on that distant day when galaxies collided, for their power was not negligible despite their lack of know-how for a long-range combat. They must stand and fight and be destroyed – the plan, the equation, was that finely balanced. Earth was the only other planet they found that was sufficiently advanced to work with, and it was imperative that Earth should not know that she was being manipulated. She must not suspect that her plans were not her own, for a young race with its pride wounded is a dubious ally and an in-effective fighting mechanism.

The Rerma set to work – willing even to die for a future they had already lived. The scientists of Rerma came secretly to Earth, and behind them, light-years away, their crystal fountains still sparkled sadly in the sun.

Rerma would be destroyed – but humanity would not die.

Conan Lang sat alone in the red room, talking to a machine. It was all clear enough, even obvious, once you knew the facts. Either there were no advanced races in the galaxy, which would account for Earth having no record of any contact – or else the Earth *had* been contacted secretly, been manipulated by the very techniques that she herself was later to use on un-developed worlds.

He looked back on history. Such profound and important changes as the Neolithic food revolution and the steam engine had been produced by Earth alone, making her the most advanced planet in the galaxy except for the Rerma. Earth had a tradition of technological skill behind her, and she was young and pliable. The Rerma came – and the so-called world wars had followed. Why? Not to avenge the honor of insulted royalty, not because of fanatics, not because of conflicting creeds – but in a very real sense to save the world. The world wars had been fought to produce atomic power.

After 1900, the development of Earth had snowballed in a fantastic manner. The atom was liberated, and man flashed upward to other planets of the solar system. Just as Conan Lang himself had worked through the ancestor gods of the Oripesh to bring about sweeping changes on Sirius Ten, the Rerma had worked through one of the gods of the Earthmen – the machine.

Cybernetics.

Man swept out to the stars, and the great thinking machines inevitably confronted them with the menace from beyond that drew nearer with each passing year. Young and proud, the men of Earth accepted the most astounding challenge ever hurled – they set out to reshape a galaxy to give their children and their children's children a chance for life.

And always, behind the scenes, beneath the headlines, were the ancient Rerma. They subtly directed and hinted and helped. With a selflessness unmatched in the universe, these representatives of a human race that had matured too far prepared Earth for galactic leadership – and themselves for death on the edge of the galaxy. They had unified Earth and pushed and prodded her along the road to survival.

When the Rerma could have fled and purchased extra time for themselves, they chose instead – these peace-loving people – to fight for another chance for man.

Conan Lang looked up, startled, to find the black figure of Fritz Gottleib standing by his side. He looked old, very old, in the blood-red light and Conan Lang looked at him with new understanding. Gottleib's impatience with others and the vast, empty loneliness in those strange eyes – all that was meaningful now. What a life that man had led on Earth, Conan Lang thought with wonder. Alone, wanting friendship and understanding - and having always to discourage close personal contacts, having always to fight his lonely battle alone in a sterile little room, knowing that the very men he had dedicated his life to help laughed behind his back and compared him to a bird of prey.

'I've been a fool, sir,' Conan Lang said, getting to his feet. 'We've all been fools.'

Fritz Gottleib sat down again behind his desk and turned the machine off. The red glow vanished, and they were left in the semidarkness.

'Not fools, Dr Lang,' he said. 'It was necessary for you to feel as you did. The feelings of one old man - what are they worth in this game we are playing? We must set our sights high, Dr Lang.'

Conan Lang waited in the shadows, thinking, watching the man who sat across from him as though seeing him for the first time. His mind was still groping, trying to assimilate all he had learned. It was a lot to swallow in a few short hours, even when you were prepared for it beforehand by guesswork and conjecture. There were still questions, of course, many questions. He knew that he still had much to learn.

'Why me?' Conan Lang asked finally. 'Why have I been told all this? Am I the only one who knows?'

Fritz Gottleib shook his head, his face ghost-white in the darkened room. 'There are others who know,' he said sibilantly. 'Your superior officer, Nelson White, has known for years of course. You were told because you have been selected to take over his command when he retires. If you are willing, you will work very closely with him here on Earth for the next five years, and then you will be in charge.'

'Will I . . . leave Earth again?'

'Not for a long time, Dr Lang. The integration-acceleration principle will keep you busy - we are in effect lifting Earth another stage, and the results will be far-reaching. But you will be home, Dr Lang - home with your family and your people.

'That is all, Dr Lang,' Gottleib hissed.

Conan Lang hesitated. 'I'll do my level best,' he said finally. 'Good-by, sir . . . I'll see you again.'

Conan Lang put out his hand to the man he had called the Buzzard and Gottleib shook it with a firm, powerful grip.

'Good-by, Conan,' Fritz Gottleib said softly.

Conan Lang turned and walked from the dark room, leaving the man from Rerma sitting alone in the shadows of the Nest.

The little bullet rose vertically on her copter blades through the evening sky, hovered a moment in the cool air under the frosty stars, and then flashed off on her jets into the west. Conan Lang set the controls and leaned back in the seat, at peace with himself at last. There *was* meaning to it all, there was a purpose - and Andy and all the others like him on the far trails had not sacrificed their lives for nothing.

Conan Lang breathed the clean air of Earth and smiled happily. Ahead of him, waiting for him, were Kit and Rob, and he would never have to leave them again. He opened the lateral ports and let the wind hurl itself at his face.

Noise

JACK VANCE

Jack Vance is a writer who enjoys working on the grand scale, producing long novellas, novels, and even clusters of novels such as his multi-paneled Demon Princes series, all marked by enormous vitality and fertility of invention. Several of the most vivid and colorful of these adventures have brought him Hugo and Nebula awards. But Vance is no less vivid, no less visionary, when he works within a smaller compass, as can be seen from this short and dream-like tale of a planet of hallucinatory beauty.

Captain Hess placed a notebook on the desk, and hauled a chair up under his sturdy buttocks. Pointing to the notebook, he said, 'That's the property of your man Evans. He left it aboard the ship.'

Galispell said in faint surprise, 'There was nothing else? No letter? We haven't heard a word from him.'

'No, sir, not a thing. That notebook was all he had when we picked him up.'

Galispell rubbed his fingers along the scarred fibers of the cover. 'It's understandable, I suppose, when you consider what he'd been through.' He flipped back the cover. 'Hmmmm.'

Hess said tentatively, 'I suppose – you've always thought of Evans as, well, rather a strange chap?'

'Howard Evans? No, not at all. He's been a very valuable man to us.' He considered Captain Hess reflectively. 'Exactly how do you mean "strange"?'

Hess frowned, searching for the precise picture of Evans' behavior. 'I guess you might say erratic, or maybe emotional.'

Galispell was genuinely startled. 'Howard Evans?'

Hess's eyes went to the notebook. 'I took the liberty of looking through his log, and – well – '

'And you got the impression he was – strange.'

Hess flushed stubbornly. 'Maybe everything he writes is true. But I've been poking into odd corners of space all my life, and I've never seen anything like it.'

'Peculiar situation,' said Galispell in a neutral voice. He looked thoughtfully at the note book.

JOURNAL OF HOWARD CHARLES EVANS

I commence this journal without pessimism but certainly without optimism. I feel as if I have already died once. My time in the lifeboat was at least a foretaste of death. I flew on and on through the dark, and a coffin could be only slightly more cramped. The stars were above, below, ahead, astern. I have no clock, and I can put no duration to my drifting. It was more than a week, it was less than a year.

So much for space, the lifeboat, the stars. There are not too many pages in this journal. I will need them all to chronicle my life on this world which, rising up under me, gave me life.

There is much to tell and many ways in the telling. There is myself, my own response to this rather dramatic situation. But lacking the knack for tracing the contours and contortions of my psyche, I will try to detail events as objectively as possible.

I landed the lifeboat on as favorable a spot as I had opportunity to select. I tested the atmosphere, temperature, pressure, and biology; then I ventured outside. I rigged an antenna and dispatched my first SOS.

Shelter is no problem; the lifeboat serves me as a bed and, if necessary, a refuge. From sheer boredom later on I may fell a few of these trees and build a house. But I will wait; there is no urgency.

A stream of pure water trickles past the lifeboat; I have abundant concentrated food. As soon as the hydroponic tanks begin to produce, there will be fresh fruits and vegetables and yeast proteins –

Survival seems no particular problem.

The sun is a ball of dark crimson, and casts hardly more light than the full moon on Earth. The lifeboat rests on a meadow of thick black-green creeper, very pleasant underfoot. A hundred yards distant in the direction I shall call south lies a lake of inky water, and the meadow slopes smoothly down to the water's edge. Tall sprays of rather pallid vegetation –

I had best use the word 'trees' – bound the meadow on either side.

Behind is a hillside, which possibly continues into a range of mountains; I can't be sure. This dim red light makes vision uncertain after the first few hundred feet.

The whole effect is one of haunted desolation and peace. I I would enjoy the beauty of the situation if it were not for the uncertainties of the future.

The breeze drifts across the lake, smelling pleasantly fragrant, and it carries a whisper of sound from off the waves.

I have assembled the hydroponic tanks, and set out cultures of yeast. I shall never starve or die of thirst. The lake is smooth and inviting; perhaps in time I will build a little boat. The water is warm, but I dare not swim. What could be more terrible than to be seized from below and dragged under?

There is probably no basis for my misgivings. I have seen no animal life of any kind: no birds, fish, insects, crustacea. The world is one of absolute quiet, except for the whispering breeze.

The scarlet sun hangs in the sky, remaining in place during many of my sleeps. I see it is slowly westering; after this long day how long and how monotonous will be the night!

I have sent off four SOS sequences; somewhere a monitor station must catch them.

A machete is my only weapon, and I have been reluctant to venture far from the lifeboat. Today (if I may use the word) I took my courage in my hands and started around the lake. The trees are rather like birches, tall and supple. I think the bark and leaves would shine a clear silver in light other than this wine-colored gloom. Along the lake shore they stand in line, almost as if long ago they had been planted by a wandering gardener. The tall branches sway in the breeze, glinting scarlet with purple overtones, a strange and wonderful picture which I am alone to see.

I have heard it said that enjoyment of beauty is magnified in the presence of others: that a mysterious rapport comes into play to reveal subtleties which a single mind is unable to grasp. Certainly as I walked along the avenue of trees with the lake and the scarlet sun behind, I would have been grateful for companionship – but I believe that something of peace, the sense of walking in an ancient abandoned garden, would be lost.

The lake is shaped like an hour-glass; at the narrow waist I could look across and see the squat shape of the lifeboat. I sat down under a bush, which continually nodded red and black flowers in front of me.

Mist fibrils drifted across the lake, and the wind made low musical sounds.

I rose to my feet and continued around the lake.

I passed through forests and glades and came once more to my lifeboat.

I went to tend my hydroponic tanks, and I think the yeast has been disturbed, prodded at curiously.

The dark red sun is sinking. Every day – it must be clear that I use 'day' as the interval between my sleeps – finds it lower in the sky. Night is almost upon me, long night. How shall I spend my time in the dark?

I have no gauge other than my mind, but the breeze seems colder. It brings long mournful chords to my ears, very sad, very sweet. Mist-wraiths go fleeting across the meadow.

Wan stars already show themselves, nameless ghostlamps without significance.

I have been considering the slope behind my meadow; tomorrow I think I will make the ascent.

I have plotted the position of every article I possess. I will be gone some hours, and – if a visitor meddles with my goods, I will know his presence for certain.

The sun is low, the air pinches at my cheeks. I must hurry if I wish to return while light still shows me the landscape. I picture myself lost; I see myself wandering the face of this world, groping for my precious lifeboat, my tanks, my meadow.

Anxiety, curiosity, obstinacy all spurring me, I set off up the slope at a half-trot.

Becoming winded almost at once, I slowed my pace. The turf of the lake shore had disappeared; I was walking on bare rocks and lichen. Below me the meadow became a patch, my lifeboat a gleaming spindle. I watched for a moment. Nothing stirred anywhere in my range of vision.

I continued up the slope and finally breasted the ridge. A vast rolling valley fell off below me. Across it rose a range of great mountains, rearing above me into the dark sky. The wine-colored light slanting in from the west lit the prominences, the frontal sallies and bluffs, left the valleys in gloom, an alternate sequence of red and black beginning far in the west, continuing past, far to the east.

I looked down behind me, down to my own meadow, and was hard put to find it in the fading light. Ah, there it was! And there, the lake, a sprawling hourglass. Beyond was dark forest, then a strip of old rose savannah, then a dark strip of woodland, then delicate laminae of colorings to the horizon.

The sun touched the edge of the mountains, and with what seemed almost a sudden lurch, fell half below the horizon. I turned down-slope; a terrible thing to be lost in the dark. My eye fell upon a white object, a hundred yards along the ridge. I stared, and walked nearer. Gradually it assumed form: a thimble, a cone, a pyramid – a cairn of white rocks. I walked forward with feet achingly heavy.

A cairn, certainly. I stood looking down on it.

I turned, looked swiftly over my shoulder. Nothing in view. I looked down to the meadow. Swift shapes? I strained through the gathering murk. Nothing.

I tore at the cairn, threw rocks aside. What was below? Nothing.

In the ground a faintly marked rectangle three feet long was perceptible. I stood back. No power I knew of could induce me to dig into that soil.

The sun was disappearing. Already at the south and north the afterglow began, lees of wine: the sun moved with astounding rapidity; what manner of sun was this, dawdling at the meridian, plunging below the horizon?

I turned down-slope, but darkness came faster. The scarlet sun was gone; in the west was the sad sketch of departed flame. I stumbled, I fell. I looked into the east. A marvelous zodiacal light was forming, a strengthening blue triangle.

I watched, from my hands and knees. A cusp of bright blue lifted into the sky. A moment later a flood of sapphire washed the landscape. A new sun of intense indigo rose into the sky.

The world was the same and yet different; where my eyes had been accustomed to red, and the multitudinous red sub-colors, now I saw the intricate cycle of blue.

When I returned to my meadow, the breeze carried a new sound: bright allegro chords that my mind could almost form into melody. For a moment I so amused myself, and thought to see dance-motion in the wisps of vapor which for the last few days had been noticeable over my meadow.

In what I will call a peculiar frame of mind, I crawled into the lifeboat and went to sleep.

I crawled blinking out of the lifeboat into an electric world. I listened. Surely that was music – faint whispers drifting in on the wind like a fragrance.

I went down to the lake, as blue as a ball of that cobalt dye so aptly known as bluing.

The music came louder; I could catch snatches of melody – sprightly quickstep phrases carried on a flowing legato like colored tinsel on a flow of cream.

I put my hands to my ears; if I was experiencing auditory hallucinations, the music would continue. The sound – if it was music – diminished, but did not fade entirely; my test was not definitive. But I felt sure it was real. And where music was there must be musicians . . . I ran forward, shouted, 'Hello!'

'Hello!' came the echo from across the lake.

The music faded a moment, as a cricket chorus quiets when disturbed, then gradually I could hear it again – distant music, 'horns of Elfland faintly blowing'.

It went completely out of perception. I was left standing haggard in the blue light, alone on my meadow.

I washed my face, returned to the lifeboat, sent out another set of SOS signals.

Possibly the blue day is shorter than the red day; with no clock I can't be sure. But with my new fascination, the music and its source, the blue day seems to pass more swiftly.

Never have I caught sight of the musicians. Is the sound generated by the trees, by diaphanous insects crouching out of my vision?

One day I glanced across the lake, and wonder of wonders! a gay town spread along the opposite shore. After a first dumbfounded gaze, I ran down to the water's edge, stared as if it were the most precious sight of my life.

Pale silk swayed and rippled: pavilions, tents, fantastic edifices. . . . Who inhabited these places? I waded kneedeep into the lake, the breath catching and creaking in my throat, and thought to see flitting shapes.

I ran like a madman around the shore. Plants with pale blue

blossoms succumbed to my feet; I left the trail of an elephant through a patch of delicate reeds.

And when I came panting and exhausted to the shore opposite my meadow, what was there? Nothing.

The city had vanished like a dream, like specters blown on a wind. I sat down on a rock. Music came clear for an instant, as if a door had momentarily opened.

I jumped to my feet. Nothing to be seen. I looked back across the lake. There – on my meadow – a host of gauzy shapes moved like May flies over a still pond.

When I returned, my meadow was vacant. The shore across the lake was bare.

So goes the blue day; and now there is fascination to my life. Whence comes the music? Who and what are these flitting shapes, never quite real but never entirely out of mind? Four times an hour I press a hand to my forehead, fearing the symptoms of a mind turning in on itself . . . If music actually exists on this world, actually vibrates the air, why should it come to my ears as Earth music? These chords I hear might be struck on familiar instruments; the progressions and harmonies are not at all alien. . . . And these pale plasmic wisps that I forever seem to catch from the corner of my eye: the semblance and style is that of gay and playful humanity. The tempo of their movement is the tempo of the music: tarantella, saraband, farandole. . . .

So goes the blue day. Blue air, blue-black turf, ultramarine water, and the bright blue star bent to the west. . . . How long have I lived on this planet? I have broadcast the SOS sequence until now the batteries hiss with exhaustion; soon there will be an end to power. Food, water are no problem to me, but what use is a lifetime of exile on a world of blue and red?

The blue day is at its close. I would like to mount the slope and watch the glory of the blue sun's passing – but the remembrance of the red sunset still provokes a queasiness in my stomach. So I will watch from my meadow, and then, if there is darkness, I will crawl into the lifeboat like a bear into a cave, and await the coming of light.

The blue day goes. The sapphire sun wanders into the western forest, the sky looms to blue-black, the stars show like unfamiliar home places.

For some time now I have heard no music; perhaps it has been so all-present that I neglect it.

The blue star is gone, the air chills. I think that deep night is on me indeed. . . . I hear a throb of sound, plangent, plaintive; I turn my head. The east glows pale pearl. A silver globe floats up into the night like a lotus drifting on a lake: a great ball like six of Earth's full moons. Is this a sun, a satellite, a burnt-out star? What a freak of cosmology I have chanced upon!

The silver sun – I must call it a sun, although it casts a cool satin light – moves in an aureolelike oyster shell. Once again the color of the planet changes. The lake glistens like quicksilver, the trees are hammered metal. . . . The silver star passes over a high rack of clouds, and the music seems to burst forth as if somewhere someone flung wide curtains: the music of moonlight, medieval marble, piazzas with slim fluted colonnades, soft sighing strains that Claude Debussy might have conceived.

I wander down to the lake. Across on the opposite shore once more I see the town. It seems clearer, more substantial; I note details that shimmered away to vagueness before – a wide terrace beside the lake, spiral pilasters, a row of decorative urns. The silhouette is, I think, the same as when I saw it under the blue sun: great silken tents, shimmering, reflecting cusps of light; pillars of carved stone, lucent as milk-glass; fantastic fixtures of no obvious purpose. . . . Barges drift along the dark quicksilver lake like moths, great sails bellying idly, the rigging a mesh of cobweb. Nodules of light, like fairy lanterns, hang on the stays, along the masts. . . . On sudden thought, I turn, look up to my own meadow. I see a row of booths as at an old-time fair, a circle of pale stone set in the turf, a host of filmy shapes.

Step by step I edge toward my lifeboat. The music waxes, chords and structures of wonderful sweetness. I peer at one of the shapes, but the outlines waver. It moves to the emotion of the music – or does the motion of the shapes generate the music?

I run forward, shouting hoarsely. One of the shapes slips past me, and I look into a blur where a face might be. I come to a halt, panting hard; I stand on the marble circle. I stamp; it rings solid. I walk toward the booths, they seem to display complex things of pale cloth and dim metal – but as I look my eyes mist over as with tears. The music goes far, far away,

64

my meadow lies bare and quiet. My feet press into silver-black turf; in the sky hangs the silver-black star.

I am sitting with my back to the lifeboat, staring across the lake, which is still as a mirror. I have arrived at a set of theories.

My primary proposition is that I am sane – a necessary article of faith; why bother even to speculate otherwise? So – events occurring outside my own mind cause everything I have seen and heard. But – note this! – these sights and sounds do not obey the laws of classical science; in many respects they seem particularly subjective.

It must be, I tell myself, that both objectivity and subjectivity enter into the situation. I receive impressions which my brain finds unfamiliar, and so translates to the concept most closely related. By this theory the inhabitants of this world are constantly close; I move unknowingly through their palaces and arcades; they dance incessantly around me. As my mind gains sensitivity, I verge upon rapport with their way of life and I see them. More exactly, I sense something which creates an image in the visual region of my brain. Their emotions, the pattern of their life set up a kind of vibration which sounds in my brain as music. . . . The reality of these creatures I am sure I will never know. They are diaphane, I am flesh; they live in a world of spirit, I plod the turf with my heavy feet.

These last days I have neglected to broadcast the SOS. Small lack; the batteries are about done.

The silver sun is at the zenith, and leans westward. What comes next? Back to the red sun? Or darkness? Certainly this is no ordinary planetary system; the course of this world along its orbit must resemble one of the pre-Copernican epicycles.

I believe that my brain is gradually tuning into phase with this world, reaching a new high level of sensitivity. If my theory is correct, the *élan vital* of the native beings expresses itself in my brain as music. On Earth we would perhaps use the word telepathy. . . . So I am practicing, concentrating, opening my consciousness wide to these new perceptions. Ocean mariners know a trick of never looking directly at a far light lest it strike the eyes' blind spot. I am using a similar device of never staring directly at one of the gauzy beings. I allow the image to establish itself, build itself up, and by this technique they appear quite definitely human. I sometimes think I can

5   65

glimpse the features. The women are like sylphs, achingly beautiful; the men – I have not seen one in detail, but their carriage, their form, is hauntingly familiar.

The music is always part of the background, just as rustling of leaves is part of a forest. The mood of these creatures seems to change with their sun, so I hear interpretive music to suit. The red sun gave them passionate melancholy, the blue sun merriment. Under the silver star they are delicate, imaginative, wistful, and in my mind sounds Debussy's *La Mer* and *Les Sirénes*.

The silver day is on the wane. Today I sat beside the lake with the trees before me like a screen of silver filigree, watching the moth-barges drift back and forth. What is their function, I wonder? Can life such as this be translated in terms of economies, ecology, sociology? I doubt it. The word 'intelligence' may not even enter the picture; is not our brain a peculiarly anthropoid characteristic, and is not intelligence a function of our peculiarly anthropoid brain? A portly barge sways near, with swamp-globes of orange and blue in the rigging, and I forget my hypotheses. I can never know the truth, and it is perfectly possible that these creatures are no more aware of me than I originally was aware of them.

Time goes by; I return to the lifeboat. A young woman-shape whirls past. I pause, peer into her face; she tilts her head, her eyes burn into mine as she passes, mocking topaz, not unkindly. . . . I try an SOS – listlessly, because I suspect the batteries to be dank and dead.

And indeed they are.

The silver star is like an enormous Christmas tree bauble, round and glistening. It floats low, and once more I stand irresolute, half expecting night.

The star falls; the forest receives it. The sky dulls, and night has come.

I face the east, my back pressed to the pragmatic hull of my lifeboat. Nothing.

I have no conception of the passage of time. Darkness, timelessness. Somewhere clocks turn minute hands, second hands, hour hands – I stand staring into the night, perhaps as slow as a sandstone statue, perhaps as feverish as a salamander.

In the darkness there is a peculiar cessation of sound. The

66

music has dwindled, down through a series of wistful chords, a forlorn last cry. . . .

A glow in the east, a green glow, spreading. Up rises a magnificent green sphere, the essence of all green, the tincture of emeralds, glowing as grass, fresh as mint, deep as the sea.

A throb of sound, music: rhythmical strong music, swinging and veering.

The green light floods the planet, and I prepare for the green day.

I am almost one with the native things. I wander among their pavilions, I pause by their booths to ponder their stuffs and wares: silken medallions, spangles and circlets of woven metal, cups of fluff and iridescent puff, puddles of color and wafts of light-shot gauze. There are chains of green glass, each link shaped like a horseshoe; captive butterflies; spheres which seem to hold all the heavens, all the clouds, all the stars.

And to all sides of me goes the flicker and flit of the dream-people. The men are all vague, but familiar; the women turn me smiles of ineffable provocation. But I will drive myself mad with temptations; what I see is no more than the formulation of my own brain, an interpretation. . . . And this is tragedy, for there is one creature so unutterably lovely that whenever I see the shape that is she, my throat aches and I run forward, to peer into her eyes that are not eyes. . . .

Today I clasped my arms around her, expecting yielding wisp. Surprisingly there was the feel of supple flesh. I kissed her, cheek, chin, mouth. Such a look of perplexity on the sweet face as I have never seen. Heaven knows what strange act the creature thought me to be performing.

She went her way, but the music is strong and triumphant: the voice of cornets, the shudder of resonant bass below.

A man comes past; something in his stride, his posture, plucks at my memory. I resolutely step forward; I will gaze into his face, I will plumb the vagueness.

He whirls past like a figure on a carousel; he wears flapping ribbons of silk and pompoms of spangled satin. I pound after him, I plant myself in his path. He strides past with a side glance, and I stare into the rigid mask-like face.

It is my own face.

He wears my face, he walks with my stride. He is me.

Already is the green day gone?

The green sun goes, and the music takes on depth. No cessation now; there is preparation, imminence. . . . What is that other sound? A far spasm of something growling and clashing like a broken gear-box.

It fades out.

The green sun goes down in a sky like a peacock's tail. The music is slow, exalted.

The west fades, the east glows. The music goes toward the east, to the great bands of rose, yellow, orange, lavender. Cloud flecks burst into flame. A golden glow consumes the sky, north and south.

The music takes on volume, a liturgical chanting.

Up rises the new sun – a gorgeous golden ball. The music swells into a paean of light, fulfillment, regeneration. . . . Hark! a second time the harsh sound grates across the music.

Into the sky, across the sun, drifts the shape of a spaceship. It hovers over my meadow, the landing jets come down like plumes.

The ship lands.

I hear the mutter of voices – men's voices.

The music is vanished; the marble carvings, the tinsel booths, the wonderful silken cities are gone.

Galispell looked up, rubbed his chin.

Captain Hess asked anxiously, 'What do you think of it?'

For a moment Galispell made no reply; then he said, 'It's a strange document. . . . ' He looked for a long moment out the window. 'What happened after you picked him up? Did you see any of these phenomena he talks about?'

'Not a thing.' Captain Hess solemnly shook his big round head. 'Sure, the system was a fantastic gaggle of dark stars and fluorescent planets and burnt-out old suns; maybe all these things played hob with his mind. He didn't seem too overjoyed to see us, that's a fact – just stood there, staring at us as if we were trespassers. "We got your SOS," I told him. "Jump aboard, wrap yourself around a good meal!" He came walking forward as if his feet were dead.

'Well, to make a long story short, he finally came aboard. We loaded on his lifeboat and took off.

'During the voyage back, he had nothing to do with anybody – just kept to himself, walking up and down the promenade.

'He had a habit of putting his hands to his head: one time I asked him if he was sick, if he wanted the medic to look him over. He said no, there was nothing wrong with him. That's about all I know of the man.

'We made Sun, and came down toward Earth. Personally, I didn't see what happened, because I was on the bridge, but this is what they tell me:

'As Earth got bigger and bigger Evans began to act more restless than usual, wincing and turning his head back and forth. When we were about a thousand miles out, he gave a kind of furious jump.

' "The noise"! he yelled. "The horrible *noise!*" And with that he ran astern, jumped into his lifeboat, cast off, and they tell me he disappeared back the way we came.

'And that's all I got to tell you, Mr Galispell. It's too bad, after our taking all that trouble to get him. Evans decided to pull up stakes – but that's the way it goes.'

'He took off back along your course?'

'That's right. If you're wanting to ask, could he have made the planet where we found him, the answer is, not likely.'

'But there's a chance?' persisted Galispell.

'Oh, sure,' said Captain Hess. 'There's a chance.'

Life Hutch

HARLAN ELLISON

Here is a tight, tense, and ingenious story of conflict aboard a rescue station in the far reaches of space – an early but thoroughly professional piece by the dynamic and turbulent Harlan Ellison, many-times winner of the Hugo and Nebula awards and editor of the impressive Dangerous Visions *anthology series.*

Terrence slid his right hand, the one out of sight of the robot, up his side. The razoring pain of the three broken ribs caused his eyes to widen momentarily in pain.

If the eyeballs click, I'm dead, thought Terrence.

The intricate murmurings of the life hutch around him brought back the immediacy of his situation. His eyes again fastened on the medicine cabinet clamped to the wall next to the robot's duty-niche.

Cliché. So near yet so far. It could be all the way back on Antares-Base for all the good it's doing me, he thought, and a crazy laugh trembled on his lips. He caught himself just in time. *Easy! Three days is a nightmare, but cracking up will only make it end sooner.*

He flexed the fingers of his right hand. It was all he *could* move. Silently he damned the technician who had passed the robot through. Or the politician who had let inferior robots get placed in the life hutches so he could get a rake-off from the government contract. Or the repairman who hadn't bothered checking closely his last time around. All of them; he damned them all.

They deserved it.

He was dying.

He let his eyes close completely, let the sounds of the life hutch fade from around him. Slowly the sound of the coolants hush-hushing through the wall-pipes, the relay machines feeding without pause their messages from all over the Galaxy, the whirr of the antenna's standard turning in its socket atop the bubble, slowly they melted into silence. He had resorted to blocking himself off from reality many times during the past three days. It was either that or exist with the robot watching, and eventually he would have had to move. To move was to die. It was that simple.

He closed his ears to the whisperings of the life hutch; he listened to the whisperings within himself.

To his mind came the sounds of war, across the gulf of space. It was all imagination, yet he could clearly detect the hiss of his scout's blaster as it poured beam after beam into the lead ship of the Kyben fleet.

His sniper-class scout had been near the face of that deadly Terran phalanx, driving like a wedge at the alien ships, converging on them in loose battle-formation. It was then it had happened.

One moment he had been heading into the middle of the battle, the left flank of the giant Kyben dreadnaught turning crimson under the impact of his firepower.

The next moment, he had skittered out of the formation which had slowed to let the Kyben craft come in closer, while the Earthmen decelerated to pick up maneuverability.

He had gone on at the old level and velocity, directly into the forward guns of a toadstool-shaped Kyben destroyer.

The first beam had burned the gun-mounts and directional equipment off the front of the ship, scorching down the aft side in a smear like oxidized chrome plate. He had managed to avoid the second beam.

His radio contact had been brief; he was going to make it back to Antares-Base if he could. If not, the formation would be listening for his homing-beam from a life hutch on whatever planetoid he might find for a crash landing.

Which was what he had done. The charts had said the pebble spinning there was technically 1–333, 2–A, M & S, 3–804.39 ♯, which would have meant nothing but three-dimensional co-ordinates, had not the small ♯ after the data indicated a life hutch somewhere on its surface.

His distaste for being knocked out of the fighting, being forced onto one of the life hutch planetoids, had been offset only by his fear of running out of fuel before he could locate himself. Of eventually drifting off into space somewhere, to finally wind up as an artificial satellite around some minor sun.

The ship pancaked in under minimal reverse drive, bounced high and skittered along, tearing out chunks of the rear section; but had come to rest a scant two miles from the life hutch, jammed into the rocks.

Terrence had high-leaped the two miles across the empty, airless planetoid to the hermetically sealed bubble in the rocks. His primary wish was to set the hutch's beacon signal so his returning fleet could track him.

He had let himself into the decompression chamber, palmed the switch through his thick spacesuit glove, and finally removed his helmet as he heard the air whistle into the chamber.

He had pulled off his gloves, opened the inner door and entered the life hutch itself.

God bless you, little life hutch, Terrence had thought as he dropped the helmet and gloves. He had glanced around, noting the relay machines, picking up messages from outside, sorting them, vectoring them off in other directions. He had seen the medicine chest clamped onto the wall, the refrigerator he knew would be well stocked if a previous tenant hadn't been there before the stockman could refill it. He had seen the all-purpose robot, immobile in its duty-niche. And the wall chronometer, its face smashed. All of it in a second's glance.

God bless, too, the gentlemen who thought up the idea of these little rescue stations, stuck all over the place for just such emergencies as this. He had started to walk across the room.

It was at this point that the service robot, who kept the place in repair between tenants and unloaded supplies from the ships, had moved clankingly across the floor, and with one fearful smash of a steel arm thrown Terrence across the room.

The spaceman had been brought up short against the steel bulkhead, pain blossoming in his back, his side, his arms and legs. The machine's blow had instantly broken three of his ribs. He lay there for a moment, unable to move. For a few seconds he was too stunned to breathe, and it had been that, perhaps, that saved his life. His pain had immobilized him, and in that short space of time the robot had retreated, with a muted internal clash of gears, to its niche.

He had attempted to sit up straight, and the robot had hummed oddly and begun to move. He had stopped the movement. The robot had settled back.

Twice more had convinced him his position was as bad as he had thought.

The robot had worn down somewhere in its printed circuits. Its commands distorted so that now it was conditioned to smash, to hit, anything that moved.

He had seen the clock. He realized he should have suspected something was wrong when he saw its smashed face. Of course! The hands had moved, the robot had smashed the clock. Terrence had moved, the robot had smashed him.

And would again, if he moved again.

But for the unnoticeable movement of his eyelids, he had not moved in three days.

He had tried moving toward the decompression lock, stopping when the robot advanced and letting it settle back, then moving again, a little nearer. But the idea died with his first movement. The agonizing pain of the crushed ribs made such maneuvering impossible. He was frozen into position, an uncomfortable, twisted position, and he would be there till the stalemate ended, one way or the other.

He was twelve feet away from the communications panel, twelve feet away from the beacon that would guide his rescuers to him. Before he died of his wounds, before he starved to death, before the robot crushed him. It could have been twelve light-years, for all the difference it made.

What had gone wrong with the robot? Time to think was cheap. The robot could detect movement, but thinking was still possible. Not that it could help, but it was possible.

The companies who supplied the life hutch's needs were all government contracted. Somewhere along the line someone had thrown in impure steel or calibrated the circuit-cutting machines for a less expensive job. Somewhere along the line someone had not run the robot through its paces correctly. Somewhere along the line someone had committed murder.

He opened his eyes again. Only the barest fraction of opening. Any more and the robot would sense the movement of his eyelids. That would be fatal.

He looked at the machine.

It was not, strictly speaking, a robot. It was merely a remote-controlled hunk of jointed steel, invaluable for making beds, stacking steel plating, watching culture dishes, unloading spaceships and sucking dirt from rugs. The robot body, roughly humanoid, but without what would have been a head in a human, was merely an appendage.

The real brain, a complex maze of plastic screens and printed circuits, was behind the wall. It would have been too dangerous to install those delicate parts in a heavy-duty mechanism. It was all too easy for the robot to drop itself from a loading shaft, or be hit by a meteorite, or get caught under a wrecked spaceship. So there were sensitive units in the robot appendage that 'saw' and 'heard' what was going on, and relayed them to the brain – behind the wall.

And somewhere along the line that brain had worn grooves too deeply into its circuits. It was now mad. Not mad in any way a human being might go mad, for there were an infinite number of ways a machine could go insane. Just mad enough to kill Terrence.

Even if I could *hit the robot with something*, *it wouldn't stop the thing*. He could perhaps throw something at the machine before it could get to him, but it would do no good. The robot brain would still be intact, and the appendage would continue to function. It was hopeless.

He stared at the massive hands of the robot. It seemed he could see his own blood on the jointed work-tool fingers of one hand. He knew it must be his imagination, but the idea persisted. He flexed the fingers of his hidden hand.

Three days had left him weak and dizzy from hunger. His head was light and his eyes burned steadily. He had been lying in his own filth till he no longer noticed the discomfort. His side ached and throbbed, the pain like a hot spear thrust into him every time he breathed.

He thanked God his spacesuit was still on, else his breathing would have brought the robot down on him. There was only one solution, and that solution was his death.

Terrence had never been a coward, nor had he been a hero. He was one of the men who fight wars because they must be fought by someone. He was the kind of man who would allow himself to be torn from wife and home and flung into an abyss they called Space because of something else they called Loyalty and another they called Patriotism. To defend what he had been told needed defense. But it was in moments like this that a man like Terrence began to think.

Why here? Why like this? What have I done that I should

74

finish in a filthy spacesuit on a lost rock – and not gloriously but starving or bleeding to death alone with a crazy robot? Why me? Why me? Why?

He knew there could be no answers. He expected no answers.

He was not disappointed.

When he awoke, he instinctively looked at the clock. Its shattered face looked back at him, jarring him, forcing his eyes open in after-sleep terror. The robot hummed and emitted a spark. He kept his eyes open. The humming ceased. His eyes began to burn. He knew he couldn't keep them open too long.

The burning worked its way to the front of his eyes, from the top and bottom, bringing with it tears. It felt as though someone were shoving needles into the soft orbs. The tears ran down over his cheeks.

His eyes snapped shut. The roaring grew in his ears. The robot didn't make a sound.

Could it be inoperative? Could it have worn down to immobility? Could he take the chance of experimenting?

He slid down to a more comfortable position. The robot charged forward the instant he moved. He froze in mid-movement, his heart a lump of snow. The robot stopped, confused, a scant ten inches from his outstretched foot. The machine hummed to itself, the noise of it coming both from the machine before him and from somewhere behind the wall.

He was suddenly alert.

If it had been working correctly, there would have been little or no sound from the appendage, and none whatsoever from the brain. But it was not working properly, and the sound of its thinking was distinct.

The robot rolled backward, its 'eyes' still toward Terrence. The sense orbs of the machine were in the torso, giving the machine the look of a squat gargoyle of metal, squared and deadly.

The humming was growing louder, every now and then a sharp *pfffft!* of sparks mixed with it. Terrence had a moment's horror at the thought of a short circuit, a fire in the life hutch, and no service robot to put it out.

He listened carefully to figure out where the robot's brain was built into the wall.

Then he thought he had it. Or was it there? It was either in the wall behind a bulkhead next to the refrigerator, or behind a bulkhead near the relay machines. The two possible housings were within a few feet of each other, but it might make a great deal of difference.

The distortion created by the steel plate in front of the brain, and the distracting background noise of the robot broadcasting it made it difficult to tell exactly which was it.

He drew a deep breath.

The ribs slid a fraction of an inch together, their broken ends grinding.

He moaned.

A high-pitched tortured moan that died quickly, but throbbed back and forth inside his head, echoing and building itself into a paeon of sheer agony! It forced his tongue out of his mouth, limp in a corner of his lips, moving slightly. The robot rolled forward. He drew his tongue in, clamped his mouth shut, cut off the scream inside his head at its high point!

The robot stopped, rolled back to its duty-niche.

Beads of sweat broke out on his body. He could feel them trickling inside his spacesuit, inside his jumper, inside the undershirt, on his skin. The pain of the ribs was suddenly heightened by an irresistible itching.

He moved an infinitesimal bit within the suit, his outer appearance giving no indication of the movement. The itching did not subside. The more he tried to make it stop, the more he thought about not thinking about it, the worse it became. His armpits, the bends of his arms, his thighs where the tight service pants clung – suddenly too tightly – were madness. He had to scratch!

He almost started to make the movement. He stopped before he started. He knew he would never live to enjoy any relief. A laugh bubbled into his head. *God Almighty, and I always laughed at the joes who suffered with the seven-year itch, the ones who always did a little dance when they were at attention during inspection, the ones who could scratch and sigh contentedly. God, how I envy them.*

The prickling did not stop. He twisted faintly. It got worse. He took another deep breath.

The ribs sandpapered again.

This time he fainted from the pain.

'Well, Terrence, how do you like your first look at a Kyben?'

Ernie Terrence wrinkled his forehead and ran a finger up the side of his face. He looked at his Commander and shrugged. 'Fantastic things, aren't they?'

'Why fantastic?' asked Commander Foley.

'Because they're just like us. Except of course the bright yellow pigmentation and the tentacle-fingers. Other than that they're identical to a human being.'

The Commander opaqued the examination-casket and drew a cigarette from a silver case, offering the Lieutenant one. He puffed it alight, staring with one eye closed against the smoke at the younger man beside him. 'More than that, I'm afraid. Their insides look like someone had taken them out, liberally mixed them with spare parts from several other species, and thrown them back in any way that fitted conveniently. For the next twenty years we'll be knocking our heads together trying to figure out how they exist.'

Terrence grunted, rolling his unlit cigarette absently between two fingers. 'That's the least of it.'

'You're right,' agreed the Commander. 'For the next thousand years we'll be trying to figure out how they think, why they fight, what it takes to get along with them, what motivates them.'

If they let us live that long, thought Terrence.

'Why are we at war with Kyben?' he asked the older man. 'I mean really.'

'Because the Kyben want to kill every human being that can realize he's a human being.'

'What have they got against us?'

'Does it matter? Perhaps it's because our skin isn't bright yellow; perhaps it's because our fingers aren't silken and flexible; perhaps it's because our cities are too noisy for them. Perhaps a lot of perhaps. But it doesn't matter. Survival never matters until you have to survive.'

Terrence nodded. He understood. So did the Kyben. It grinned at him and drew its blaster. It fired point-blank, crimsoning the hull of the Kyben ship.

He swerved to avoid running into his gun's own backlash. The movement of the bucket seat sliding in its tracks to keep his vision steady while maneuvering made him dizzy.

The abyss was nearer, and he teetered, his lips whitening as they pressed together under his effort to steady himself. With a headlong gasp he fell sighing into the stomach. His long, silken fingers jointed steely humming clankingly toward the medicine chest over the plate behind the bulkhead.

The robot advanced on him grindingly. Small fine bits of metal rubbed together, ashing away into a breeze that came from nowhere as the machine raised lead boots toward his face.

Onward and onward till he had no room to move.

The light came on, bright, brighter than any star Terrence had ever seen, glowing, broiling, flickering, shining, bobbing a ball of light on the chest of the robot, who staggered, stumbled, stopped.

The robot hissed, hummed and exploded into a million flying, racing fragments, shooting beams of light all over the abyss over which Terrence teetered. He flailed his arms back trying to escape at the last moment, before the fall.

He saved himself only by his subconscious. Even in the hell of a nightmare he was aware of the situation. He had not moaned and writhed in his delirium. He had kept motionless and silent.

He knew this was true, because he was still alive.

Only his surprised jerking, as he came back to consciousness started the monster rolling from its niche. He came fully awake and sat silent, slumped against the wall. The robot retreated.

Thin breath came through his nostrils. Another moment and he would have put an end to the past three days – three days or more now? How long had he been asleep? – of torture.

He was hungry. Lord, how hungry he was. The pain in his side was worse now, a steady throbbing that made even shallow breathing tortuous. He itched maddeningly. He was uncomfortably slouched against a cold steel bulkhead, every rivet having made a burrow for itself in his skin. He wished he were dead.

He didn't wish he were dead. It was all too easy to get his wish.

If he could only disable that robot brain. A total impossibility. If he could only wear Phobos and Deimos for watchfobs. If he could only shack-up with a silicon-deb from Penares. If he could only use his large colon for a lasso.

It would take a total wrecking of the brain to do it enough damage to stop the appendage before it could roll over and smash Terrence again.

With a steel bulkhead between him and the brain, his chances of success totaled minus zero every time.

He considered which part of his body the robot would smash first. One blow of that tool-hand would kill him if it were used a second time. On top of the ribs, even a strong breath might finish him.

Perhaps he could make a break and get into the air chamber . . .

Worthless. (a) The robot would catch him before he had gotten to his feet, in his present condition. (b) Even allowing for a miracle, if he did get in there, the robot would smash the lock doors, letting in air, ruining the mechanism. (c) Even allowing for a double miracle, what the hell good would it do him? His helmet and gloves were in the hutch itself, and there was no place to go on the planetoid. The ship was ruined, so no signal could be sent from there.

Doom suddenly compounded itself.

The more he thought about it, the more certain he was that soon the light would flicker out for him.

The light would flicker out.

The light would flicker . . .

The light . . .

. . . light . . . ?

His God, if he had had anything to do with it, had heard him. Terrence was by no means a religious man, but this was miracle enough to make even him a disciple. It wasn't over yet, but the answer was there – and it *was* an answer.

He began to save himself.

Slowly, achingly slowly, he moved his right hand, the hand away from the robot's sight, to his belt. On the belt hung the assorted implements a spaceman needs at any moment in his ship. A wrench. A packet of sleep-stavers. A compass. A geiger counter. A flashlight.

The last was the miracle. Miracle in a tube.

He fingered it almost reverently, then unclipped it in a moment's frenzy, still immobile to the robot's 'eyes'.

He held it at his side, away from his body by a fraction of an inch, pointing up over the bulge of his space-suited leg.

If the robot looked at him, all it would see would be the motionless bulk of his leg, blocking off any movement on his part. To the machine, he was inert. Motionless.

Now, he thought wildly, *where is the brain?*

If it is behind the relay machines, I'm still dead. If it is near the refrigerator, I'm saved. He could afford to take no chances. He would have to move.

He lifted one leg.

The robot moved toward him. The humming and sparking was distinct this time. He dropped the leg.

Behind the plates above the refrigerator!

The robot stopped, nearly at his side. Seconds had decided. The robot hummed, sparked, and returned to its niche.

Now he knew!

He pressed the button. The invisible beam of the flashlight leaped out, speared at the bulkhead above the refrigerator. He pressed the button again and again, the flat circle of light appearing, disappearing, appearing, disappearing on the faceless metal of the life hutch's wall.

The robot sparked and rolled from its niche. It looked once at Terrence. Then its rollers changed direction and the machine ground toward the refrigerator.

The steel fist swung in a vicious arc, smashing with a deafening clang at the spot where the light bubble flickered on and off.

It swung again and again. Again and again till the bulkhead had been gouged and crushed and opened, and the delicate coils and plates and wires and tubes behind it were refuse and rubble. Until the robot froze, with arm half-ready to strike again. Dead. Immobile. Brain and appendage.

Even then Terrence did not stop pressing the flashlight button. Wildly he thumbed it down and down.

Suddenly he realized it was all over.

The robot was dead. He was alive. He would be saved. He had no doubts about that. *Now* he could cry.

The medicine chest grew large through the shimmering in his eyes. The relay machines smiled at him.

God bless you, little life hutch, he thought, before he fainted.

Ticket to Anywhere

DAMON KNIGHT

Even so far-reaching a transportation system as the New York subways offers only a relatively limited number of choices of destination: uptown or downtown, Brooklyn or the Bronx, East Side or West Side. But how does one cope with a system that offers every passenger the whole universe? Damon Knight examines some of the implications of such a cosmic express with his characteristic grace and thoughtfulness.

Richard Falk was a sane man. Up until three months ago he had been, so far as he could discover, the only sane man left in a world of lunatics.

Now he was a dead man.

He lay in a metal coffin twenty yards long by three wide, airless, soundless. Behind the faceplate of his helmet, under the rime of frozen air, his lips were bright blue, his cheeks, nose, forehead a lighter color, almost violet. The flesh was stiff as frozen leather. He did not move, breathe, or think: he was dead.

Beside him, strapped to the bulging torso of his suit, was a metal box labeled 'SCATO HEART PROBE. SEE INSTRUCTIONS INSIDE.'

All around him, strapped tight to the walls by broad loops of webbing, were boxes, canisters, canvas bags, kegs. Cargo. His coffin was a freighter, going to Mars.

In his frozen brain the memories were neatly stacked, just as he had left them. Not coupled now, each cell isolated, the entropy of his mind fallen to zero. But uppermost among them, waiting for the thaw that might never come, were the memories of his last few hours of life.

Once the ship was launched and free, he had had to wait until its dancing molecules had stilled, their heat all radiated away into space. Then to wait again, heater turned off, listening to the silence while his own life's heat drained away: fingers and toes numb first, ears and nose following, then lips, cheeks, and all his flesh; shivering in an agony of cold, watching his breath fill the helmet with cloud, the cold drops beading on the colder faceplate.

Tricky, that, and a thing that demanded courage. Act too soon, and the last drop into stillness would be too slow – the freezing liquids in his body would crystallize, gashing his cells with a million tiny stabs. Wait too long, and the cold would steal his ability to act at all.

He had waited until the false warmth of the dying had crept over him, the subtle destroyer, cumbering his limbs not with harshness but with too much peace. Twisting then in the dead center where he floated, he had drawn himself into the lane between two looped bundles of cargo, forcing them aside, until he reached the naked hull. There, spread-eagled against the chill metal, embracing it as one who crucifies himself gladly, he had died.

The ship, stillest of sepulchers, hung fixed in the center of the starry globe. So it might have remained for time without end, changeless, knowing no time; for there was no time here, no 'events' – the ship and all its contents – except its robot control, inactive now but warmed by a minute trickle of electrons – now being very nearly at zero Absolute.

But a relay clicked, communicating its tremor through support frame and girder and hull. Time had begun again. The radar assembly in the prow began to emit timed clusters of radiation; presently other relays snapped over, and then the engine awoke, whispered to itself an instant, and was silent. For an instant the ship had become once more a thing in motion, a pebble flung between the stars. Another such instant came, then another; then, at long last, the hull shuddered to the whip and carom of atmospheric molecules. Lightly it dipped into Martian air, out again, in again, making a great circuit of the globe. A final relay clicked, and Falk's coffin hurled itself groundward, free of the skeletal ship whose rockets now flamed again, driving it back into the timeless deep.

A parachute opened as the cargo hull hurtled downward: a preposterous parasol that would not have held the weight a minute against Earth's gravity, in Earth's air; but here it slowed that plummeting fall until the box met Martian sand at not quite killing speed.

In the shell, Falk's corpse slowly thawed.

His heart was beating. That was Falk's first conscious realization, and he listened to the tiny sound thankfully. His chest was rising and falling in a deep, slow rhythm; he heard the hiss and whisper of breath in his nostrils and felt the veins twitch at his temples.

Then came a prickling, half pain, in his arms and legs; then he saw a ruddy haze of light on his closed lids.

Falk opened his eyes.

He saw a pale glow that turned itself into a face. It went away briefly, then came back. Falk could see it a little better now. Young – about thirty – pale-skinned, with a blue beard shadow. Black straight hair, a little untidy. Black-rimmed spectacles. Ironic lines on either side of the thin mouth.

'All right now?' said the face.

Falk murmured, and the face bent closer. He tried again. 'Think so.'

The young man nodded. He picked up something from the bed and began taking it apart, fitting the components into the cushioned troughs of a metal box. It was the heart probe, Falk saw: the bulky control box and the short, capillary-thin needle.

'Where did you get this?' the young man asked. 'And what the devil were you doing aboard that freighter?'

'Stole the probe,' said Falk. 'And the suit, and the rest of the stuff. Dumped enough cargo to match my weight. Wanted to get to Mars. Only way.'

The young man let his hands fall into his lap. 'You *stole* it,' he repeated incredulously. 'Then you never had the analogue treatment?'

Falk smiled. 'Had it, all right. Dozen times. Never took.' He felt very tired. 'Let me rest a minute, will you?'

'Of course. Sorry.'

The young man went away, and Falk closed his eyes, returning to the slow surge of memory that moved in his mind. He went through those last hours, painful as they were, and then again. There was trauma there; mustn't let it get buried to cause him trouble later. Accept it, know the fear, live with it.

After a while the young man came back, carrying broth that

steamed in a cup, and Falk drank it gratefully. Then he fell unknowing into sleep.

When he awoke he was stronger. He tried to sit up, and found to his mild surprise that he could. The other, who had been sitting in an armchair across the room, put down his pipe and came over to thrust pillows behind Falk's back. Then he sat down again. The room was cluttered and had a stale odor. Floor, walls and ceiling were enameled metal. There were books and rolls of tape, records, in shelves; more piled on the floor. A dirty shirt was hanging from the doorknob.

'Want to talk now?' the young man asked. 'My name's Wolfert.'

'Glad to know you. Mine's Falk. . . . You want to know about the analogue business first, I suppose.'

'And why you're here.'

'It's the same thing,' Falk told him. 'I'm immune to analogue treatment. I didn't know it for sure till I was ten, but I think I was born that way. From seven on, I remember the other kids talking about their Guardians, and me pretending I had one too. You know how kids are – anything to run with the mob.

'But for a long time, years, I wasn't certain whether everyone else was pretending like me, or whether I really was the only one without an invisible Guardian to talk to. I was pretty sure the kids were lying when they said they could see theirs, but whether they were there at all or not was another question. I didn't know; actually it didn't bother me much.

'When I was ten, I stole something. It was a book I wanted that my father wouldn't let me have. The clerk was looking the other way – I put it under my jacket. Funny, I was halfway through it before it struck me that I'd just proved I had no Guardian. By that time, you see, I'd decided that I'd just never seen mine because I'd never done anything bad. I was proud of that, a little prissy about it, if you want the truth – only I wanted this book. . . .

'I had sense enough, thank God, to burn that book after I'd finished it. If I hadn't, I don't suppose I would have lived to grow up.'

Wolfert grunted. 'Should think not,' he said. His eyes were fixed on Falk, interested, alert, wary. 'One man without any control could turn the whole applecart over. But I thought immunity was theoretically impossible?'

'I've thought about that a good deal. According to classic psychology, it is. I'm not unusually resistant to hypnotic drugs; I go under all right. But the censor mechanism just doesn't respond. I've had the fanciful notion that I may be a mutation, developed in response to the analogue treatment as an antisurvival factor. But I don't know. As far as I've ever been able to find out, there are no more like me.'

'Umm,' said Wolfert, puffing at his pipe. 'Should think your next move would be to get married, have children, see if they were immune too.'

Falk stared at him soberly. 'Wolfert – no offense, but can you imagine yourself settling down happily in a community of maniacs?'

The other's face flushed slowly. He took the pipe out of his mouth, looked down at it. Finally he said, 'All right, I know what you mean.'

'Maybe you don't,' said Falk, thinking, *I've offended him. Couldn't help it.* 'You've been out here ten years, haven't you?'

Wolfert nodded.

'Things are getting worse,' Falk told him. 'I've taken the trouble to look up some statistics. They weren't hard to find; the damned fools are proud of them. The number of persons in mental institutions has gone steadily down since 1980, when the world-wide analogue program got under way. Extension of analogue program, steadily up. The two curves cancel out perfectly.

'There are fewer and fewer people that have to be put away in madhouses – not because of any improvement in therapy, but because the analogue techniques are getting better and better. The guy who would have been hopelessly insane fifty years ago now has a little man inside his head, steering him around, making him act normal. On the outside he *is* normal; inside, he's a raving madman. Worse still, the guy who would have been just a little bit cracked fifty years ago – and gotten treatment for it – is now just as mad as the first guy. It doesn't matter any more. We could all be maniacs, and the world would go on just as before.'

Wolfert grimaced wryly. 'Well? It's a peaceful world, anyhow.'

'Sure,' said Falk. 'No war or possibility of war, no murders, no theft, no crime at all. That's because every one of them has a policeman inside his skull. But action begets reaction,

Wolfert, in psychiatry as well as in physics. A prison is a place to get out of, if it takes you a lifetime. Push one plunger down, another will rise. Just a few years more, I think – ten or twenty, say – and you'll see that madhouse curve rise again. Because there's no escape from the repression of the Guardians except a further retreat into insanity. And eventually a point is reached where no amount of treatment can help. What are they going to do then?'

Wolfert tamped his pipe out slowly and stood up, sucking absently at the stem. 'You say *they*,' he said, 'meaning the psychiatrists who really govern Earth, I suppose. You've evidently figured out what you're going to do.'

Falk smiled. 'Yes. With your help – I'm going to the stars.'

The other stood frozen a moment. 'So you know about that,' he said. 'Well – Come into the next room. I'll show it to you.'

Falk had known about the Doorway, but not that it looked like this. It was a cubicle of something that looked like slick brown glass. Ten feet high, six wide and deep. Inside, at waist level on the far wall, a lever – curiously shaped, like the head of an old-fashioned walking stick, the slightly curved bar of the L parallel to the wall. Nothing more than that. The floor of Wolfert's hut had been assembled around it. It was the reason for the hut's existence, for Wolfert's dearly bought presence on Mars.

'So that's it,' said Falk. He took a step toward it.

'Stay where you are,' Wolfert said sharply. 'The area in front of the entrance is booby-trapped.'

Falk stopped and looked at Wolfert, then at the metal cabinets bolted to the floor on either side of the Doorway. Now that he looked at them closely, he could see the lenses of black-light beams and, above them, metal cones that he supposed were discharge points.

Wolfert confirmed it. 'If anything ever comes out, the current is supposed to get him. If it doesn't, I'm here.' He put his hand on the rapid-fire automatic at his belt.

Falk sat down slowly on a bench next to the wall. 'Why?' he asked. 'Why are they so afraid of whatever might come out of the Doorway?'

The other leaned awkwardly against the wall and began refilling his pipe. 'You don't know the whole story, then,' he said. 'Tell me what you do know, and I'll fill in the gaps.'

Falk said slowly, 'I was able to find out that the Doorway

86

existed – that the first Mars expedition, in '76, had found it here. Apparently it was known to be an interstellar transportation system, but as far as I could learn nobody had ever actually tried it out. I knew that a caretaker had been left here – your predecessor, I take it – after the idea of colonizing Mars was abandoned. But I didn't know any of the reasons.'

Wolfert grinned briefly and straightened away from the wall. As he talked, he paced back and forth across the room, glancing at Falk only occasionally. 'It's a transportation system, all right. Put an object in that cubicle, press the lever down – the object vanishes. So does most of the crowbar or whatever you use to work the lever. *Ffft* – gone.

'We don't know how old it is and have no way of telling. The material it's made of is harder than diamond. About half of it is underground. That was the way it was found – sitting perfectly level on the surface of the desert. I believe it must have some sort of self-leveling mechanism built into it so that it's always available no matter what happens to the surface.

'Other ruins have been found on Mars, but they're all stone and quite primitive, nothing like this. The first expedition tried to get into its innards and find out what made it go, of course, but they couldn't. You can *see* in, but there's nothing to see.' He gave his quick, bitter smile. 'It's frustrating. Makes a physicist feel like a backward student in a kindergarten.

'We know that it's part of an interstellar network. One man did try it out – a member of the first expedition, one of the group that found the Doorway in the first place. He saw the cubicle and the lever – stepped in and pressed it to find out what would happen. *He* found out, all right, but I don't suppose the rest of us will ever know. The second expedition brought along a batch of powerful all-wave senders and sent them through. They picked up the first signal five years later, from the general direction of Regulus. Two more after seven years, then four during the thirteenth year, all from different directions. The other eight have yet to be heard from.'

He stopped pacing and looked at Falk. 'Now do you understand? The thing has no selectivity – it's completely random. We could walk through there and step out onto the planet of another star, all right – but it would take us a million years to find the way back by trial and error.' He knocked his pipe out against the heel of his hand, letting the dottle fall on the floor. 'There it sits, the doorway to the stars. And we can't use it.'

Falk leaned back against the wall, trying to absorb the idea. 'Maybe there are only a dozen or so stars in the network,' he suggested.

Wolfert's thin mouth drew down at the corners. 'Don't be a fool,' he said. 'Would the race that could build *that*' – he gestured toward the cubicle – 'stop at a dozen stars, or a thousand? The devil! They owned the galaxy!' Nervously he began to fill his pipe again. 'Sixty billion stars,' he said. 'And according to current theory, all the mainliners have planets.'

He pointed to the cubicle again. 'Three hundred sixty cubic feet, about,' he said. 'Enough for one man and supplies for a month, or fifteen people and supplies for a week. That's the limit of the size of the colony we could send out. With no assurance,' he added bitterly, 'that they'd land anywhere they could live for a minute.'

'Frustrating,' Falk agreed. 'But I still don't see why you're here – with a gun. I can understand that if a member of the race that built that thing came through – and I must say it seems unlikely – that would be an important event. But why kill him when he steps out?'

'Dammit,' said Wolfert violently, 'it isn't my policy, Falk. I only work here.'

'I understand that,' Falk said. 'But do you have any idea what's behind the policy?'

'Fear,' said Wolfert promptly. 'They've got too much at stake.' He leaned against the wall again, gesturing with his pipestem. 'Do you realize,' he said, 'that we could have interstellar colonization *without* this gadget, on our own? Certainly. Not now, but fifty, a hundred years from now – if we worked at it. Give us a fuel source efficient enough so that we can accelerate continuously for as long as eight months, and we could reach the stars well within a man's lifetime. But do you know why we won't?'

'They're afraid. They're even afraid to plant colonies here on Mars, or on Jupiter's moons, simply because transportation takes too long. Imagine a colony cut off from Earth by a five- or ten-year trip. Say something goes wrong – a man like yourself, naturally immune to analogue treatment. Or a man who somehow evades the treatment, then manages to take it over, change it. Say he cuts out the one directive, "You must do nothing against the policy or interests of Earth." Then you've got two communities again, not one. And then – ?'

Falk nodded soberly. 'War. I see now. They don't dare take even the smallest chance of that.'

'It isn't a question of daring, they *can't*. That's one of the directives in their own conditioning, Falk.'

'So we'll never get to the stars.'

'Unless,' said Wolfert, 'somebody walks out of that Doorway who understands how it works. The voltage is high, but not high enough to kill – we hope. He's supposed to be stunned. If the current doesn't stop him, and he tries to get back into the Doorway, I'm supposed to shoot to cripple. But at all events, he's supposed to be stopped. He isn't to be allowed to go back and warn others to stay away from this station. Because if we had that knowledge – how to alter the system so that it would be selective – '

'Then we'd have colonies, all right,' finished Falk. 'Everyone just around the corner from Earth. All just alike. The loonies shall inherit the Universe. . . . I hope nobody ever comes through.'

'I don't think you're likely to be disappointed,' said Wolfert.

II

He prowled the rest of the cabin with Wolfert, resting at intervals until his strength returned. There wasn't much to see: the Doorway room, with a spyhole Falk had not noticed between it and the bedroom; the room that housed radio, radar, and the computer that controlled the grazing orbits of the supply rockets; the power plant, and the compressor that kept the cabin's air at breathable pressure; kitchen, bathroom, and two storage chambers.

The radio room had a window, and Falk stood there a long time, looking out over the alien desert, violet now as the sun dropped toward the horizon. Stars glittered with unfamiliar brilliance in the near-black sky, and Falk found his gaze drawn to them even against the tug of that unearthly landscape.

In his mind he sketched hairlines of fire across the sky – a cat's cradle of stars. The thought that tomorrow he would be standing on a planet of one of those suns was like an icy douche; the mind recoiled from it as from the thought of personal death. But at the same time it lured him. He felt like a boy standing on the edge of an unsounded pool whose black waters might hold treasure or death: he was afraid to dive, and yet he knew that he must.

How could a man feel otherwise, he wondered, knowing that the way was open, that he had only to step forward?

Wolfert said abruptly, 'You haven't asked me whether I reported to Earth when I found you in that freighter shell.'

Falk looked at him. 'You did, of course,' he said. 'It doesn't matter. I'll be gone long before they can do anything about me. You'll tell them that I overpowered you and escaped through the Doorway – they won't be able to prove otherwise – unless you're conditioned against lying?'

'No,' said Wolfert, 'I'm not. That part's all right, with one emendation: I'll say I revived you, then shot and buried you. But what made you so sure that I'd be – sympathetic?'

'You're here,' said Falk simply. 'You're a volunteer. They haven't got to the stage of conditioning people to do jobs they don't want to do, though I suppose they will eventually. And when I'd heard you speak, I knew you were intelligent. So – you're a hermit. You don't like the madhouse they're making out of Earth, any more than I do.'

'I don't know,' said Wolfert slowly. 'Perhaps you're assuming too much similarity.' He looked down at his everpresent pipe, tamping the tobacco with a horny thumb: 'I don't feel as you do about the analogue system, or the present government. I'm – adjusted, there. In my personal universe, it works. I can see that it will lead to disaster eventually, but that doesn't bother me much. I'll be dead.'

He looked at Falk earnestly. 'But I want the stars,' he said. 'That's an emotional thing with me. . . . There are no slugs in these cartridges.' He indicated the gun at his hip. 'Or in any of the ammunition I've got. They didn't condition me against that.'

Falk stared at him. 'Look,' he said abruptly, 'you've got a directive against stepping through that Doorway, is that right?'

The other nodded.

'Well, but is there any reason why I couldn't knock you over the head and drag you through?'

Wolfert smiled wryly, shaking his head slowly. 'No good,' he said. 'Somebody's got to stay, this end.'

'Why?'

'Because there's a chance that you'll find the secret out there, somewhere. That's what you're hoping, too, isn't it? You're not just looking for a place to hide – you could do that in a thousand places on Earth. You're after knowledge, and in spite of what I've told you, you're hoping you'll be able to bring it back and make the Earth over.'

'It sounds a little quixotic,' said Falk, 'but you're right.'

Wolfert shrugged, letting his gaze drift away again. 'Well, then . . . there's got to be somebody here. Somebody with no slugs in his gun. If I went with you, they'd take good care to send a different sort of man next time.'

He met Falk's eyes again briefly. 'Don't waste time feeling sorry for me,' he said. 'You may not believe it, but I'm quite happy here. When I'm . . . alone, that is.'

Falk had been wondering why the government had not sent a married couple instead of a single man, who might go mad from sheer loneliness. Now it struck him that he had been stupid. Wolfert had a wife, undoubtedly; the best kind – one who suited him perfectly, who would never be fickle, or want to return to Earth; one who cost nothing to feed, consumed no air, and had not added an ounce of weight when Wolfert had been shipped out here. And on Mars it did not ordinarily matter that no one else could see her.

He felt an inward twinge of revulsion and instantly knew that Wolfert had seen and understood it. The man's cheeks flushed, and he turned away to stare through the window, his lips thin and hard.

After a moment Falk said, 'Wolfert, I like you better than any man I've ever met. I hope you'll believe that.'

Wolfert hauled out a pipe cleaner, a complicated thing of many hinged stems, the free ends stamped into shovel shapes, tamper shapes, probes. He said, 'I'm afraid I dislike you, Falk, but it's nothing personal. I simply hate your guts a little, because you've got something I wasn't lucky enough to be born with. You're the master of your own mind.'

He turned and put out his hand, grinning. 'Aside from that trifling matter, I entirely approve of you. If that's good enough – ?'

Falk gripped his hand. 'I hope you're here when I get back,' he said.

'I'll be here,' said Wolfert, scraping his pipe, 'for another thirty-odd years, barring accidents. If you're not back by then, I don't suppose you'll be coming back at all.'

At Wolfert's suggestion, Falk put on one of the other's light Mars suits instead of the spacesuit he had worn in the freighter. The latter, designed for heavy-duty service in the orbital space station that circled Earth, was, as Wolfert pointed out, too clumsy for use on a planet's surface. The lighter suit furnished adequate protection in thin atmosphere and was equipped with gadgetry that the other lacked: a head lamp, climbing gear, built-in compass, and traps for the occupant's ingestion and excretion. It carried air tanks, but also had a compression outfit – which, given an atmosphere at least as oxygen-rich as that of Mars, would keep the wearer alive for as long as the batteries held out.

'You'll have to find a place where you can live off the land, so to speak, anyhow,' said Wolfert. 'If all the planets you hit should happen to be dead, so will you be, very shortly. But this suit will give you longer to look, at least, and the stuff in the knapsack will last you as long as you have air. I'd give you this gun, but it wouldn't do you any good – all the ammunition's buggered, as I told you.'

He disconnected the booby trap and stood aside as Falk moved to the entrance. Falk took one last look around at the bare metal room and at Wolfert's spare figure and gloomy face. He stepped into the brown glass cubicle and put his gloved hand on the lever.

'See you later,' he said.

Wolfert nodded soberly, almost indifferently. 'So long, Falk,' he said, and put his pipe back in his mouth.

Falk turned on his helmet lamp, put his free hand near the control box at his belt – and pressed the lever down.

Wolfert vanished. An instant later Falk was aware that the lever was no longer beneath his hand. He turned, dazedly, and saw that it was back in its original position, above his hand.

Then he remembered the curious blank that had taken Wolfert's place and he turned again to the entrance. He saw – nothing. A gray-white blankness, featureless, uncommunicative. Was this some kind of intermediary state – and if so, how long did it last? Falk felt a brief surge of panic as he realized they had only assumed the journey was instantaneous, and another as he recalled the eight transmitters that had never been heard from. . . .

Then common sense took over, and he stepped forward to the entrance.

The gray-white shaded gradually, as his gaze traveled downward, into gray-blue and violet, and then a chaos of dim colors of which his eye made nothing. He gripped the edge of the Doorway and bent forward, looking downward and still downward. Then he saw the cliff, and all the rest of the scene fell into perspective.

He stood at the top of a sheer mountain – an impossible, ridiculous height. Down it went and again down, until whatever was at the bottom melted into a meaningless tapestry of grayed color. He looked to right and left and saw nothing else. No sound came through the diaphragm of his helmet. He had only the tactile and muscular responses of his own body, and the hard reality of the Doorway itself, to assure him that he was real and live.

The planet was dead; he felt irrationally sure of that. It *felt* dead; there was not even a whisper of wind: only the featureless blanket of gray cloud, the cliff, the meaningless colors below.

He looked at the kit slung to his belt: the pressure gauge, bottled litmus papers, matches. But there was no point in testing this atmosphere: even if it were breathable, there was clearly no way of getting out of the Doorway. The cliff began not more than an inch from the entrance.

Falk went back to the lever, pressed it down again.

This time he watched it as it reached the end of its stroke. There was no hint of a transition: the lever was there, under his hand, and then it was back in the starting position – as if it had passed unfelt through the flesh of his hand.

He turned.

Deep blue night, blazing with stars. Underneath, a flat blue-green waste that ran straight away into the far distance.

Falk stepped out onto the icy plain and looked around him, then upward. The sky was so like the one he had known as a boy in Michigan that it struck him almost as a conviction that this terminus was on Earth – in the Antarctic, perhaps, near the pole, where no explorer had ever happened across it. Then, as he looked automatically for the Dipper, Orion's Belt, he knew that he was wrong.

He saw none of the familiar patterns. These were alien stars, in an alien sky. He reviewed what he could remember of the configurations of Earth's southern hemisphere, but none of them fitted either.

Directly above him was a group of eight stars, two of them very brilliant – four arranged in a straight line, the rest spread out in an almost perfect semicircle. Falk knew that if he had ever seen that constellation before he would not have forgotten it.

Now he looked down toward the horizon, blacker than the sky. How could he know that light, warmth, safety, knowledge were not hiding just beyond the curve of the planet?

He turned back to the cubicle. He was here on sufferance, a man in a Mars suit, with weeks – or, with great luck, months or years – to live. He had to find what he sought within a pitifully small radius from the Doorway, or not at all.

Down went the lever again. Now it was still night – but when Falk went to the Doorway, he saw an avenue of great buildings under the stars.

Now the pressure gauge came out – low, but the compressor could handle it. The litmus papers – negative. The match burned – weakly, and only for an instant, but it burned.

Falk started the compressor and shut off the flow of air from the tanks slung at his back. Then he turned on his helmet light and marched off down the avenue.

The buildings were variations on a theme: pyramid, cone, and wedge shape, they sloped away as they rose, so that for all their enormous bulk they did not hide the sky. Falk looked up when he had taken a few steps, subconsciously expecting to see the half-circle constellation. But it was not there, and he realized with a shock that, for all he knew, he might be halfway across the galaxy from the spot where he had stood five minutes ago.

He drew a picture of the galaxy in his mind, an oval clot of mist against blackness. Near one focus of the ellipse he put a dot of brightness that stood for Sol. Then he made another dot and drew a shining line between them. Then another dot, and another line; then another. They made a sprawling letter N across the misty oval.

It was incomprehensible. A race that could span the galaxy, but could not choose one destination from another?

The only other alternative was this: there was some function of the Doorways that men had failed to grasp, some method of selection that evaded them, as a savage might be bewildered in a modern tubeway system. But Falk's mind rejected that. The mechanism was simple and clear. A cubicle and a lever. Function is expressed by shape; and the shape of the Doorway said 'Go'; it did not say 'Where?'

He looked again at the buildings. The upper quarter of them, he saw now, was badly eroded: layers inches deep had been eaten away. He glanced at the fine orange sand that paved the avenue and saw that it filled doorways almost to the top. Evidently this city had lain all but buried for many years, and in some recent time the shifting sands had uncovered it again.

The space between the sand and the tops of the doorways was narrow, but he thought he could squeeze through. He picked out one, centering it in the brilliant disk of his head lamp – and stood there, in the middle of the avenue, reluctant to move.

He glanced back at the cubicle, as if for reassurance. It was still there, comfortably clear and sharp-lined, timeless. Now he realized what was troubling him. This city was dead – dead as the planet of the cliff or the planet of ice. The buildings were stone; they had crumbled under the weather. Their makers were dust.

He had agreed with Wolfert when the other had suggested that he was on a quest for knowledge; that he hoped the Doorway would eventually take him back to Sol, armed with knowledge, ready to remake the world. But it wasn't true. That had been his conscious idea, but it was a dream, a self-delusion – an excuse.

He had no love for Earth, or any conviction that humanity must be rescued from its own weakness. If that force had driven him, there would have been no logic in leaving Earth. He could have stayed, worked himself into the governing elite, organized a revolution from within. His chance of success would have been small, but there would have been some chance.

Yes, he might have done it – and for what? To remove the one control that kept humanity from destroying itself?

That coin had the same face on both sides. Uncontrolled, mankind was not fit to colonize. Controlled, it dared not take the risk. Human civilization was not ready, was a dead end, an aborted experiment. Mankind was a dirty beast, ravaging its planet, defouling itself – capable of any imaginable perversion, degradation, horror.

But there had been another civilization once – one that had been worthy of the stars. Falk did not believe it was dead. Stone crumbled; metal rusted; and the races that used them vanished and were not mourned. The Doorways still lived, still functioned, defying time.

That race was not here; it had left no trace of itself except the Doorway. Without another glance at the buildings around him, Falk turned and went back to the brown glass cubicle.

When he was three yards away from it, he saw the footprints.

There were five of them, lightly impressed into the sand near the Doorway's entrance. Search as he might, Falk could not find any more. Two, apparently, pointed away from the cubicle; the other three were the returning trail, for one overlapped one of the previous set.

They were smaller than Falk's booted prints, oval, slightly flattened along the sides. Falk stared at them as if the mere act of looking would make them give up more information; but they told him nothing.

They were not human; but what did that prove?

They had been made long since the time when the Doorways had been built; Falk did not know what winds swept this world, but it could only have been a few years, at most, since the sands had dropped to their present level. But even that train of logic led nowhere.

They could be the trace of a Doorway builder. Or they could have been made by a wanderer like himself, another barbarian venturing in the paths of his betters.

The bitterest thing of all was that, having found the trail, he could not follow it. For it led through the Doorway – to any one of sixty billion suns.

Falk stepped into the cubicle and pressed the lever down once more.

III

White light that sealed his eyes with pain, and a vicious torrent of heat. Gasping, Falk groped frantically for the lever.

The afterimage faded slowly. He saw night again, and the stars. That last one, he thought, must have been the planet of a nova. How many of those was he likely to run into?

He stepped to the doorway. A wasteland: not a stick, not a stone.

He went back to the lever. Light again, of bearable intensity, and a riot of color outside.

Falk stepped cautiously to the entrance. Slowly his mind adapted to the unfamiliar shapes and colors. He saw a bright landscape under a tropic sun – gray-violet mountains in the distance, half veiled by mist; nearer, tall stalks that bore heavy leaves and fronds of a startling blue-green; and directly ahead of him, a broad plaza that might have been cut from one monstrous boulder of jade. On either side were low, box-shaped structures of dark vitreous material: blue, brown, green, and red. And in the middle of the plaza stood a group of slender shapes that were unquestionably alive, sentient.

Falk's heart was pounding. He stepped behind the shelter of the entrance wall and peered out. Curiously it was not the cluster of live things that drew him, but the buildings on either side.

They were made of the same enduring, clean-edged substance as the Doorway. He had come, by blind chance, at last to the right place.

Now he stared at the creatures grouped in the middle of the plaza. For some reason they were disappointing. They were slender S-shapes, graceful enough in repose: lizard shapes, upright on two legs; pink of belly and umber of back. But in spite of the bandoliers slung from their narrow shoulders, in spite of their quick, patterned gestures as they spoke together, Falk could not convince himself that he had found the people he sought.

They were too manlike. One turned away while two others spoke; came back leaning at a passionate angle, thrust himself between the two, gesturing wildly. Shouted down, he again left and stalked a half circle around the group. He moved as a chicken moves, awkwardly, thrusting his long neck forward at each step.

Of the five others, two argued, two merely stood with drooping, attentive heads and watched; and the last stood a little apart, gazing around him disdainfully.

They were funny, as monkeys are funny – because they

resemble men. We laughed at our mirrored selves. Even the races of man laugh at each other when they should weep.

They're tourists, Falk thought. *One wants to go to the Lido, another insists they see the Grand Canal first : the third is furious with both of them for wasting time, the next two are too timid to interfere, and the last one doesn't care.*

He couldn't imagine what their reaction to him would be. Nothing welcome, at any rate; they might want to take him home as a souvenir. He wanted to get into those buildings, but he'd have to wait until they were out of sight.

While he waited, he got out the atmosphere-testing kit. The pressure gauge showed the merest trifle less than Earth normal; the litmus papers did not react; the match burned cheerfully, just as it would have on Earth. Falk turned off the oxygen, cracked the helmet valve cautiously, and sniffed.

After the stale air of the suit, the breath he inhaled was so good that it brought tears to his eyes. It was fresh, faintly warm, and sweet with flower fragrance. Falk opened the helmet seam, tipped the helmet back, and let the breeze wash over his face and hair.

He peered out, and saw to his dismay that that the party was trooping directly toward him. Falk ducked his head back inside, glanced instinctively at the lever, then looked out again.

They were running now; they had seen him. They ran very clumsily, heads darting strenuously forward and back. The one in the lead was opening and shutting his triangular mouth, and Falk heard faint yawps. He leaped out of the cubicle, cut sharply to the right, and ran.

The nearest building with a visible opening, unfortunately, was some distance down the line, between Falk and the lizards. He glanced back when he was halfway there. The lizards were considerably strung out now, but the leader was only a few yards away.

They were faster than they looked. Falk put his head down and tried to make his heavy boots move to a quicker rhythm. Almost to the door, he looked back again. The lizard was one jump away, its grimy, ball-tipped fingers outspread.

Falk turned in desperation and, as the lizard came up, swung a knotted fist to the point of its snout. He heard its steam-whistle screech, saw it collapse, and then he was diving through the open door ahead.

The door closed gently behind him – a sheet of glassy substance, the same blue as the walls, gliding down to seal the opening.

Falk stared at it. Through its transparency he could see the dark shapes of the lizards crowding around, leaning to pry at the bottom of the door, gesticulating at each other. It was plain, at any rate, that the door was not going to open for them.

Whether it would open for him, when he wanted it to, was another matter.

He looked around him. The building was a single huge room, so long and deep that he could barely see the far walls. Scattered over the floor, patternless, were boxes, or chests, racks, shelves, little ambiguous mounds. Nearly all the objects Falk could see were fashioned of the same glasslike material.

There was no dust in the room; but now that Falk thought of it, he realized that there had been none in any of the Door-ways, either. How that was done he could not conjecture. He moved to the nearest object, a file, or rack formed apparently to take many things of divers shapes and sizes. It was a quarter empty now, and the remaining contents had a jumbled look.

He picked up an orange glass spindle, full of embedded threads, or flaws that looped in a curious pattern from one end to the other. He put it down, took a hollow sphere of opal. It was made in halves and seemed to be empty, but Falk could find no way to take it apart. He replaced it and took a brown object shaped like a double crescent, with a clear fracture plane running diagonally through it. . . .

Half an hour later he realized that he was not going to find any picture books or engineering manuals or any one thing that would unlock the mystery of the Doorway people for him. If there were any knowledge to be gained here, it would have to come from the building as a whole.

The lizards distracted him. He could see them through the walls of the building, pressing their snouts against the glass, staring with little round eyes, gesturing at him. But he learned things from them.

The group broke up finally, leaving only one to guard the exit; the others dispersed. Falk saw one go into the building directly across the plaza. The door closed behind him. A little later another one approached and pounded on the door; but it did not open until the first lizard came close to it inside. Some automatic mechanism, beyond Falk's fathoming, evidently responded to the presence or absence of any living thing inside each building. When the last person left, the door stayed open; when another person entered, it shut and would not open for the next unless the first person allowed it.

That added one item to the description of the Doorway people that Falk was building in his mind. They were not property-conscious – not afraid that thieves would enter in their absence, for the doors stood open when they were gone – but they respected each other's love of privacy.

Falk had previously thought of this building as a vast factory or laboratory or dormitory – a place designed to serve a large number of people, anyhow. Now he revised his opinion. Each building, he thought, was the private domain of one person – or, if they had family groups, only two or three. But how could one person use all this space, all these possessions?

He made the comparison that by now was becoming automatic. He asked himself what a cliff dweller would make of a millionaire's triplex apartment in New York.

It helped, but not enough. The objects around him were all specialized tools; they would not function for him and so told him nothing about the Doorway builders. There was nothing that he could compare to a bed, to a table, to a shower bath. He could not see the people who had lived here.

With an effort, he forced himself to stop thinking in terms of men. The facts were important, not his prejudices. And then what had been a barrier became a road. There were no beds, tables, showers? Then the Doorway people did not sleep; they did not eat; they did not bathe.

Probably, thought Falk, they did not die.

They were fit to live among the stars. . . .

The riddle of the deserted chamber mocked him. How, having built this city, would they leave it? How would they spread the network of the Doorways across the face of the galaxy, and then leave it unused?

The first question answered itself. Looking at the littered chamber, Falk thought of his comparison of the cliff dweller and the millionaire and humbly acknowledged his presumption. Not a millionaire's triplex, he told himself . . . a tent.

Once there had been something of particular interest on this world. No telling what it had been, for that had been some millions of years ago when Mars was a living world. But the Doorway people, a few of them, had come here to observe it. When they were finished, they had gone away, leaving their tents behind, as a man might abandon a crude shelter of sticks and leaves.

And the other things they had left behind them? The cubes, cones, rods, odd shapes, each one beyond price to a man? *Empty cans*, thought Falk; *toothpaste tubes, wrapping paper.*

They had abandoned this city and the million things in it because they were of no value.

The sun was redder, nearer the horizon. Falk looked at the chronometer strapped to the wrist of his suit and found to his surprise that it was more than five hours since he had left Wolfert on Mars.

He had not eaten. He took food out of his pack and looked at the labels on the cans. But he was not hungry; he did not even feel tired.

He watched the lizards outside. They were scurrying around in the plaza now, bringing armloads of junk from the building, packing them into big red boxes. As Falk watched, a curious construction floated into view down at the far end of the plaza. It was a kind of airboat, an open shell with two lizards riding it, supported by two winglike extensions with streamlined, down-pointing shapes at their ends.

It drifted slowly until it hovered over the pile of boxes the lizards had gathered. Then a hatch opened in its belly, and a hook emerged at the end of three cords. The lizards on the plaza began slinging loops of cord from their boxes to the hook.

Falk watched them idly. The hook began to rise, dragging the boxes after it, and at the last moment one of the lizards tossed another loop over it.

The new box was heavy; the hook stopped when it took up the slack, and the airboat dipped slightly. Then it rose again, and the hook rose too, until the whole load was ten feet off the ground.

Abruptly one of the three cords snapped; Falk saw it whip through the air, saw the load lurch ponderously to one side, and the airboat dip. Simultaneously the pilot sent the boat down to take up the strain on the remaining cords.

The lizards were scattering. The load struck heavily; and a moment later so did the airboat. It bounced, skidded wildly, and came to rest as the pilot shut off the power.

The lizards crowded around again, and the two in the air-boat climbed down for an interminable conference. Eventually they got aboard again, and the boat rose a few feet while the lizards beneath disengaged the hook. Then there was another conference. Falk could see that the doors of the boat's hatch were closed and had a crumpled look. Evidently they were jammed and could not be opened again.

Finally the boat came down once more, and with much argument and gesticulation the boxes were unpacked and some of their contents reloaded into two boxes, these being hoisted with much effort into the airboat's cockpit. The rest was left strewn around the plaza.

The airboat lifted and went away, and most of the lizards followed it. One straggler came over for a last look at Falk; he peered and gestured through the wall for a while, then gave it up and followed the rest. The plaza was deserted.

Some time passed, and then Falk saw a pillar of white flame that lifted, with a glint of silver at its tip, somewhere beyond the city, and grew until it arched upward to the zenith, dwindled, and vanished.

So they had spaceships, the lizards. They did not dare use the Doorways, either. Not fit, not fit . . . too much like men.

Falk went out into the plaza and stood, letting the freshening breeze ruffle his hair. The sun was dropping behind the mountains, and the whole sky had turned ruddy, like a great crimson cape streaming out of the west. Falk watched, reluctant to leave, until the colors faded through violet to gray, and the first stars came out.

It was a good world. A man could stay here, probably, and live his life out in comfort and ease. No doubt there were exotic fruits to be had from those trees; certainly there was water; the climate was good; and Falk thought sardonically that there could be no dangerous wild beasts, or those twittering tourists would never have come here.

If all a man wanted was a hiding place, there could be no better world than this. For a moment Falk was strongly tempted. He thought of the cold dead world he had seen and wondered if he would ever find a place as fair as this again. Also, he knew now that if the Doorway builders still lived, they must long ago have drawn in their outposts. Perhaps they lived now on only one planet, out of all the billions. Falk would die before he found it.

He looked at the rubble the lizards had left in the middle of the plaza. One box was still filled, but burst open; that was the one that had caused all the trouble. Around it was a child's litter of baubles – pretty glass toys, red, green, blue, yellow, white.

A lizard, abandoned here by his fellows, would no doubt be happy enough in the end.

With a sigh, Falk turned back to the building. The door opened before him, and he collected his belongings, fastened down his helmet, strapped on his knapsack again.

The sky was dark now, and Falk paused to look up at the familiar sweep of the Milky Way. Then he switched on his helmet light and turned toward the waiting Doorway.

The light fell across the burst box the lizards had left, and Falk saw a hard edge of something thrusting out. It was not the glassy adamant of the Doorway builders; it looked like stone.

Falk stooped and tore the box aside.

He saw a slab of rock, roughly smoothed to the shape of a wedge. On its upper face, characters were incised. They were in English.

With blood pounding in his ears, Falk knelt by the stone and read what was written there.

THE DOORWAYS STOP THE AGING PROCESS. I WAS 32 WHEN I LEFT MARS, AM HARDLY OLDER NOW THOUGH I HAVE BEEN TRAVELING FROM STAR TO STAR FOR A TIME I BELIEVE CANNOT BE LESS THAN 20 YRS. BUT YOU MUST KEEP ON. I STOPPED HERE 2 YRS. FOUND MYSELF AGING – HAVE OBSERVED THAT MILKY WAY LOOKS NEARLY THE SAME FROM ALL PLANETS SO FAR VISITED. THIS CANNOT BE COINCIDENCE. BELIEVE THAT DOORWAY TRAVEL IS RANDOM ONLY WITHIN CONCENTRIC BELTS OF STARS & THAT SOONER OR LATER YOU HIT DOORWAY WHICH GIVES ENTRY TO NEXT INNERMOST BELT. IF I AM RIGHT, FINAL DESTINATION IS CENTER OF GALAXY. I HOPE TO SEE YOU THERE.

JAMES E. TANNER
NATIVE OF EARTH

Falk stood up, blinded by the glory of the vision that grew in his mind. He thought he understood now why the Doorways were not selective and why their makers no longer used them.

Once – a billion years ago, perhaps – they must have been uncontested owners of the galaxy. But many of their worlds were small planets like Mars – too small to keep their atmospheres and their water forever. Millions of years ago, they must have begun to fall back from these. And meanwhile, Falk thought, on the greater worlds just now cooling, the lesser breeds had arisen: the crawling, brawling things. The lizards. The men. Things not worthy of the stars.

But even a man could learn if he lived long enough, journeyed far enough. James Tanner had signed himself not 'TERRAN SPACE CORPS' or 'U.S.A.' but 'NATIVE OF EARTH.'

So the way was made long, and the way was made hard; and the lesser breeds stayed on their planets. But for a man, or a lizard, who would give up all that he called 'life' for knowledge, the way was open.

Falk turned off the beam of his head lamp and looked up at the diamond mist of the galaxy. Where would he be a thousand years from today? Standing on that mote of light, or that, or that . . . ?

Not dust, at any rate. Not dust, unmourned, unworthy. He would be a voyager with a destination, and perhaps half his journey would be done.

Wolfert would wait in vain for his return, but it would not matter; Wolfert was happy – if you called that happiness. And on Earth, the mountains would rise and fall long after the question of human survival had been forgotten.

Falk, by that time, perhaps, would be home.

The Sixth Palace

ROBERT SILVERBERG

It was the richest treasure in the galaxy, and all one had to do to win it was answer a few questions. . . . But death was the penalty for the wrong sort of right answer!

Ben Azai was deemed worthy and stood at the gate of the sixth palace and saw the ethereal splendor of the pure marble plates. He opened his mouth and said twice, 'Water! Water!' In the twinkling of an eye they decapitated him and threw eleven thousand iron bars at him. This shall be a sign for all generations that no one should err at the gate of the sixth palace.

—Lester Hekhaloth

There was the treasure, and there was the guardian of the treasure. And there were the whitened bones of those who had tried in vain to make the treasure their own. Even the bones had taken on a kind of beauty, lying out there by the gate of the treasure vault, under the blazing arch of the heavens. The treasure itself lent beauty to everything near it – even the scattered bones, even the grim guardian.

The home of the treasure was a small world that belonged to red Valzar. Hardly more than moon-sized, really, with no atmosphere to speak of, a silent, dead little world that spun through darkness a billion miles from its cooling primary. A wayfarer had stopped there once. Where from, where bound? No one knew. He had established a cache there, and there it still lay, changeless and eternal, treasure beyond belief, presided over by the faceless metal man who waited with metal patience for his master's return.

There were those who would have the treasure. They came, and were challenged by the guardian, and died.

On another world of the Valzar system, men undiscouraged by the fate of their predecessors dreamed of the hoard, and schemed to possess it. Lipescu was one: a tower of a man, golden beard, fists like hammers, gullet of brass, back as broad as a tree of a thousand years. Bolzano was another: awl-shaped, bright of eye, fast of finger, twig thick, razor sharp. They had no wish to die.

Lipescu's voice was like the rumble of island galaxies in collision. He wrapped himself around a tankard of good black ale and said, 'I go tomorrow, Bolzano.'

'Is the computer ready?'

'Programmed with everything the beast could ask me,' the big man boomed. 'There won't be a slip.'

'And if there is?' Bolzano asked, peering idly into the blue, oddly pale, strangely meek eyes of the giant. 'And if the robot kills you?'

'I've dealt with robots before.'

Bolzano laughed. 'That plain is littered with bones, friend. Yours will join the rest. Great bulky bones, Lipescu. I can see them now.'

'You're a cheerful one, friend.'

'I'm realistic.'

Lipescu shook his head heavily. 'If you were realistic, you wouldn't be in this with me,' he said slowly. 'Only a dreamer would do such a thing as this.' One meaty paw hovered in the air, pounced, caught Bolzano's forearm. The little man winced as bones ground together. Lipescu said, 'You won't back out? If I die, you'll make the attempt?'

'Of course I will, you idiot.'

'Will you? You're a coward, like all little men. You'll watch me die, and then you'll turn tail and head for another part of the universe as fast as you know how. Won't you?'

'I intend to profit by your mistakes,' Bolzano said in a clear, testy voice. 'Let go of my arm.'

Lipescu released his grip. The little man sank back in his chair, rubbing his arm. He gulped ale. He grinned at his partner and raised his glass.

'To success,' Bolzano said.

'Yes. To the treasure.'

'And to long life afterward.'

'For both of us,' the big man boomed.

'Perhaps,' said Bolzano. 'Perhaps.'

He had his doubts. The big man was sly, Ferd Bolzano knew, and that was a good combination, not often found: slyness and size. Yet the risks were great. Bolzano wondered which he preferred – that Lipescu should gain the treasure on his attempt, thus assuring Bolzano of a share without risk, or that Lipescu should die, forcing Bolzano to venture his own life. Which was better, a third of the treasure without hazard, or the whole thing for the highest stake?

Bolzano was a good enough gambler to know the answer to that. Yet there was more than yellowness to the man; in his own way, he longed for the chance to risk his life on the airless treasure world.

Lipescu would go first. That was the agreement. Bolzano had stolen the computer, had turned it over to the big man, and Lipescu would make the initial attempt. If he gained the prize, his was the greater share. If he perished, it was Bolzano's moment next. An odd partnership, odd terms, but Lipescu would have it no other way, and Ferd Bolzano did not argue the point with his beefy compatriot. Lipescu would return with the treasure, or he would not return at all. There would be no middle way, they both were certain.

Bolzano spent an uneasy night. His apartment, in an airy shaft of a building overlooking glittering Lake Eris, was a comfortable place, and he had little longing to leave it. Lipescu, by preference, livened in the stinking slums beyond the southern shore of the lake, and when the two men parted for the night, they went in opposite ways. Bolzano considered bringing a woman home for the night, but did not. Instead, he sat moody and wakeful before the televector screen, watching the procession of worlds, peering at the green and gold and ocher planets as they sailed through the emptiness.

Toward dawn, he ran the tape of the treasure. Octave Merlin had made that tape, a hundred years before, as he orbited sixty miles above the surface of the airless little world. Now Merlin's bones bleached on the plain, but the tape had come home, and boot-legged copies commanded a high price in hidden markets. His camera's sharp eye had seen much.

There was the gate; there was the guardian. Gleaming, age-less, splendid. The robot stood ten feet high, a square, blocky, black shape topped by the tiny anthropomorphic head dome, featureless and sleek. Behind him the gate, wide open but impassable all the same. And behind him the treasure, culled from the craftsmanship of a thousand worlds, left here who knew why, untold years ago.

No mere jewels. No dreary slabs of so-called precious

metal. The wealth here was not intrinsic; no vandal would think of melting the treasure into dead ingots. Here were statuettes of spun iron, that seemed to move and breathe. Plaques of purest lead, engraved with lathework that dazzled the mind and made the heart hesitate. Cunning intaglios in granite, from the workshops of a frosty world half a parsec from nowhere. A scatter of opals, burning with an inner light, fashioned into artful loops of brightness.

A helix of rainbow-colored wood. A series of interlocking strips of some beast's bone, bent and splayed so that the pattern blurred and perhaps abutted some other dimensional continuum. Cleverly carved shells, one within the other, descending to infinity. Burnished leaves of nameless trees. Polished pebbles from unknown beaches. A dizzying spew of wonders, covering some fifty square yards, sprawled out behind the gate in stunning profusion.

Rough men unschooled in the tenets of aesthetics had given their lives to possess the treasure. It took no fancy knowledge to realize the wealth of it, to know that collectors strung from galaxy to galaxy would fight with bare fangs to claim their share. Gold bars did not a treasure make. But these things? Beyond duplication, almost beyond price?

Bolzano was wet with a fever of yearning before the tape had run its course. When it was over, he slumped in his chair, drained, depleted.

Dawn came. The silvery moons fell from the sky. The red sun splashed across the heavens. Bolzano allowed himself the luxury of an hour's sleep.

And then it was time to begin. . . .

As a precautionary measure, they left the ship in a parking orbit three miles above the airless world. Past reports were unreliable, and there was no telling how far the robot guardian's power extended. If Lipescu was successful, Bolzano could descend and get him – and the treasure. If Lipescu failed, Bolzano would land and make his own attempt.

The big man looked even bigger, encased in his suit and in the outer casement of a dropshaft. Against his massive chest he wore the computer, an extra brain as lovingly crafted as any object in the treasure hoard. The guardian would ask him questions; the computer would help him answer. And Bolzano would listen. If Lipescu erred, possibly his partner could benefit by knowledge of the error and succeed.

'Can you hear me?' Lipescu asked.

'Perfectly. Go on, get going!'

'What's the hurry? Eager to see me die?'

'Are you lacking in confidence?' Bolzano asked. 'Do you want me to go first?'

'Fool,' Lipescu muttered. 'Listen carefully. If I die, I don't want it to be in vain.'

'What would it matter to you?'

The bulky figure wheeled around. Bolzano could not see his partner's face, but he knew Lipescu must be scowling. The giant rumbled, 'Is life that valuable? Can't I take a risk?'

'For *my* benefit?'

'For mine,' Lipescu said. 'I'll be coming back.'

'Go, then. The robot is waiting.'

Lipescu walked to the lock. A moment later he was through and gliding downward, a one-man spaceship, jets flaring beneath his feet. Bolzano settled by the scanner to watch. A televector pickup homed in on Lipescu just as he made his landing, coming down in a blaze of fire. The treasure and its guardian lay about a mile away. Lipescu rid himself of the dropshaft, stepping with giant bounds toward the waiting guardian.

Bolzano watched.

Bolzano listened.

The televector pickup provided full fidelity. It was useful for Bolzano's purposes, and useful, too, for Lipescu's vanity, for the big man wanted his every moment taped for posterity. It was interesting to see Lipescu dwarfed by the guardian. The black faceless robot, squat and motionless, topped the big man by better than three feet.

Lipescu said, 'Step aside.'

The robot's reply came in surprisingly human tones, though void of any distinguishing accent. 'What I guard is not to be plundered.'

'I claim them by right,' Lipescu said.

'So have many others. But their right did not exist. Nor does yours. I cannot step aside for you.'

'Test me,' Lipescu said. 'See if I have the right or not!'

'Only my master may pass.'

'Who is your master? *I* am your master!'

'My master is he who can command me. And no one can command me who shows ignorance before me.'

'Test me, then,' Lipescu demanded.

'Death is the penalty for failure.'

'Test me.'

'The treasure does not belong to you.'

'Test me and step aside.'

'Your bones will join the rest here.'

'Test me,' Lipescu said.

Watching from aloft, Bolzano went tense. His thin body drew together like that of a chilled spider. Anything might happen now. The robot might propound riddles, like the Sphinx confronting Oedipus.

It might demand proofs of mathematical theorems. It might ask the translation of strange words. So they gathered, from their knowledge of what had befallen other men here. And, so it seemed, to give the wrong answer was to earn instant death.

He and Lipescu had ransacked the libraries of the world. They had packed all knowledge, so they hoped, into their computer. It had taken months, even with multistage programming. The tiny globe of metal on Lipescu's chest contained an infinity of answers to an infinity of questions.

Below, there was a long silence as man and robot studied one another. Then the guardian said, 'Define latitude.'

'Do you mean geographical latitude?' Lipescu asked.

Bolzano congealed with fear. The idiot, asking for a clarification! He would die before he began!

The robot said, 'Define latitude.'

Lipescu's voice was calm. 'The angular distance of a point on a planet's surface north or south of the equator, as measured from the center of the planet.'

'Which is more consonant,' the robot asked, 'the minor third or the major sixth?'

There was a pause. Lipescu was no musician. But the computer would feed him the answer.

'The minor third,' Lipescu said.

Without a pause, the robot fired another question. 'Name the prime numbers between five thousand two hundred and thirty-seven and seven thousand six hundred and forty-one.'

Bolzano smiled as Lipescu handled the question with ease. So far, so good. The robot had stuck to strictly factual questions, schoolbook stuff, posing no real problems to Lipescu. And after the initial hesitation and quibble over latitude, Lipescu had seemed to grow in confidence from moment to moment. Bolzano squinted at the scanner, looking beyond the robot, through the open gate, to the helter-skelter pile of treasures. He wondered which would fall to his lot when he and Lipescu divided them, two thirds for Lipescu, the rest for him.

'Name the seven tragic poets of Elifora,' the robot said.

'Domiphar, Halionis, Slegg, Hork-Sekan . . .'

'The fourteen signs of the zodiac as seen from Morneez,' the robot demanded.

'The Teeth, the Serpents, the Leaves, the Waterfall, the Blot . . .'

'What is a pedicel?'

'The stalk of an individual flower of an inflorescence.'

'How many years did the Siege of Larrina last?'

'Eight.'

'What did the flower cry in the third canto of Somner's *Vehicles*?'

' "I ache, I sob, I whimper, I die," ' Lipescu boomed.

'Distinguish between the stamen and the pistil.'

'The stamen is the pollen-producing organ of the flower; the pistil . . .'

And so it went. Question after question. The robot was not content with the legendary three questions of mythology; it asked a dozen, and then asked more. Lipescu answered perfectly, prompted by the murmuring of the peerless compendium of knowledge strapped to his chest. Bolzano kept careful count: The big man had dealt magnificently with seventeen questions. When would the robot concede defeat? When would it end its grim quiz and step aside?

It asked an eighteenth question, pathetically easy. All it wanted was an exposition of the Pythagorean theorem. Lipescu did not even need the computer for that. He answered, briefly, concisely, correctly. Bolzano was proud of his burly partner.

Then the robot struck Lipescu dead.

It happened in the flickering of an eyelid. Lipescu's voice had ceased, and he stood there, ready for the next question, but the next question did not come. Rather, a panel in the robot's vaulted belly slid open, and something bright and sinuous lashed out, uncoiling over the ten feet or so that separated guardian from challenger, and sliced Lipescu in half. The bright something slid back out of sight. Lipescu's trunk toppled to one side. His massive legs remained absurdly planted for a moment; then they crumpled, and a spacesuit leg kicked once, and all was still.

Stunned, Bolzano trembled in the loneliness of the cabin, and his lymph turned to water. What had gone wrong? Lipescu had given the proper answer to every question, and yet the robot had slain him. Why? Could the big man possibly have misphrased Pythagoras? No: Bolzano had listened. The answer had been flawless, as had the seventeen that preceded it. Seemingly the robot had lost patience with the game, then. The robot had cheated. Arbitrarily, maliciously, it had lashed out at Lipescu, punishing him for the correct answer.

Did robots cheat? Bolzano wondered. Could they act in malicious spite? No robot he knew was capable of such actions; but this robot was unlike all others.

For a long while, Bolzano remained huddled in the cabin. The temptation was strong to blast free of orbit and head home, treasureless but alive. Yet the treasure called to him. Some suicidal impulse drove him on. Sirenlike, the robot drew him downward.

There had to be a way to make the robot yield, Bolzano thought, as he guided his small ship down to the broad barren plain. Using the computer had been a good idea, whose only defect was that it hadn't worked. The records were uncertain, but it appeared that in the past, men had died when they finally gave a wrong answer after a series of right ones. Lipescu had given no wrong answers. Yet he too had died. It was inconceivable that the robot understood some relationship of the squares on the hypotenuse and on the other two sides that was different from the relationship Lipescu had expressed.

Bolzano wondered what method would work.

He plodded leadenly across the plain toward the gate and its guardian. The germ of an idea formed in him, as he walked doggedly on.

He was, he knew, condemned to death by his own greed. Only extreme agility of mind would save him from sharing Lipescu's fate. Ordinary intelligence would not work. Odyssean cleverness was the only salvation.

Bolzano approached the robot. Bones lay everywhere. Lipescu weltered in his own blood. Against that vast dead chest lay the computer, Bolzano knew. But he shrank from reaching for it. He would do without it. He looked away, unwilling to let the sight of Lipescu's severed body interfere with the coolness of his thoughts.

He collected his courage. The robot showed no interest in him.

'Give ground,' Bolzano said. 'I am here. I come for the treasure.'

'Win your right to it.'

'What must I do?'

'Demonstrate truth,' the robot said. 'Reveal inwardness. Display understanding.'

'I am ready,' said Bolzano.

The robot offered a question. 'What is the excretory unit of the vertebrate kidney called?'

Bolzano contemplated. He had no idea. The computer could tell him, but the computer lay strapped to the fallen Lipescu. No matter. The robot wanted truth, inwardness, understanding. These things were not necessarily the same as information. Lipescu had offered information. Lipescu had perished.

'The frog in the pond,' Bolzano said, 'utters an azure cry.'

There was silence. Bolzano watched the robot's front, waiting for the panel to slide open, the sinuous something to chop him in half.

The robot said, 'During the War of Dogs on Vanderverr IX, the embattled colonists drew up thirty-eight dogmas of defiance. Quote the third, the ninth, the twenty-second, and the thirty-fifth.'

Bolzano pondered. This was an alien robot, product of an unknown hand. How did its maker's mind work? Did it respect knowledge? Did it treasure facts for their own sake? Or did it recognize that information is meaningless, insight a nonlogical process?

Lipescu had been logical. He lay in pieces.

'The mereness of pain,' Bolzano responded, 'is ineffable and refreshing.'

The robot said, 'The monastery of Kwaisen was besieged by the soldiers of Oda Nobunaga on the third of April, 1582. What words of wisdom did the abbot utter?'

Bolzano spoke quickly and buoyantly: 'Eleven, forty-one, elephant, voluminous.'

The last word slipped from his lips despite an effort to retrieve it. Elephants *were* voluminous, he thought. A fatal slip? The robot did not appear to notice.

Sonorously, ponderously, the great machine delivered the next question:

'What is the percentage of oxygen in the atmosphere of Muldonar VII?'

'False witness bears a swift sword,' Bolzano replied.

The robot made an odd humming sound. Abruptly it rolled on massive treads, moving some six feet to its left. The gate of the treasure trove stood wide, beckoning.

'You may enter,' the robot said.

Bolzano's heart leaped. He had won! He had gained the high prize!

Others had failed, most recently less than an hour before, and their bones glistened on the plain. They had tried to answer the robot, sometimes, giving right answers, sometimes giving wrong ones, and they had died. Bolzano lived.

It was a miracle, he thought. Luck? Shrewdness? Some of each, he told himself. He had watched a man give eighteen right answers and die. So the accuracy of the responses did not matter to the robot. What did? Inwardness. Understanding. Truth.

There could be inwardness and understanding and truth in random answers, Bolzano realized. Where earnest striving had failed, mockery had succeeded. He had staked his life on nonsense, and the prize was his.

He staggered forward into the treasure trove. Even in the light gravity, his feet were like leaden weights. Tension ebbed in him. He knelt among the treasures.

The tapes, the sharp-eyed televector scanners, had not begun to indicate the splendor of what lay here. Bolzano stared in awe and rapture at a tiny disk, no greater in diameter than a man's eye, on which myriad coiling lines writhed and twisted in patterns of rare beauty. He caught his breath, sobbing with the pain of perception, as a gleaming marble spire, angled in mysterious swerves, came into view. Here, a bright beetle of some fragile waxy substance rested on a pedestal of yellow jade. There, a tangle of metallic cloth spurted dizzying patterns of luminescence. And over there – and beyond – and there –

The ransom of a universe, Bolzano thought.

It would take many trips to carry all this to his ship. Perhaps it would be better to bring the ship to the hoard, eh? He wondered, though, if he would lose his advantage if he stepped back through the gate. Was it possible that he would have to win entrance all over again? And would the robot accept his answers as willingly the second time? It was something he would have to chance, Bolzano decided. His nimble mind worked out a plan. He would select a dozen of the finest treasures, as much as he could comfortably carry, and take them back to the ship. Then he would lift the ship and set it down next to the gate. If the robot raised objections about his entering, Bolzano would simply depart, taking what he had already secured. There was no point in running undue risks. When he had sold this cargo, and felt pinched for money, he could always return and try to win admission once again. Certainly, no one else would steal the hoard if he abandoned it.

Selection, that was the key now.

Crouching, Bolzano picked through the treasure, choosing for portability and easy marketability. The marble spire? Too big. But the coiling disk, yes, certainly, and the beetle, of course, and this small statuette of dull hue, and the cameos showing scenes no human eye had ever beheld, and this, and this, and this –

His pulse raced. His heart thundered. He saw himself traveling from world to world, vending his wares. Collectors, museums, governments would vie with one another to have these prizes. He would let them bid each object up into the millions before he sold. And, of course, he would keep one or two for himself – or perhaps three or four – souvenirs of this great adventure.

And someday when wealth bored him he would return and face the challenge again. And he would dare the robot to question him, and he would reply with random absurdities, demonstrating his grasp of the fundamental insight that in knowledge there is only hollow merit, and the robot would admit him once more to the treasure trove.

Bolzano rose. He cradled his lovelies in his arms. Carefully, he thought. Turning, he made his way through the gate.

The robot had not moved. It had shown no interest as Bolzano plundered the hoard. The small man walked calmly past it.

The robot said, 'Why have you taken those? What do you want with them?'

Bolzano smiled. Nonchalantly he replied, 'I've taken them because they're beautiful. Because I want them. Is there a better reason?'

'No,' the robot said, and the panel slid open in its ponderous black chest.

Too late, Bolzano realized that the test had not yet ended, that the robot's question had arisen out of no idle curiosity. And this time he had replied in earnest, speaking in rational terms.

Bolzano shrieked. He saw the brightness coming toward him.

Death followed instantly.

Lulungomeena

GORDON R. DICKSON

Gordon Dickson is a hearty, outgoing Minnesotan whose long list of published stories includes the Hugo-winning 'Soldier, Ask Not,' the Nebula-award story 'Call Him Lord', and the novella 'Things Which Are Caesar's', in the omnibus collection The Day the Sun Stood Still. *His work is marked by warmth, sympathy, and insight into character – all of which are much in evidence in this account of some beings, human and otherwise, among the stars far from home.*

Blame Clay Harbank, if you will, for what happened at Station 563 of the Sirius Sector; or blame William Peterborough, whom we called the Kid. I blame no one. But I am a Dorsai man.

The trouble began the day the kid joined the station, with his quick hands and his gambler's mind, and found that Clay, alone of all the men there, would not gamble with him – for all that he claimed to have been a gambling man himself. And so it ran on for four years of service together.

But the beginning of the end was the day they came off shift together.

They had been out on a duty circuit of the frontier station that housed the twenty of us – searching the outer bubble for signs of blows or leaks. It's a slow two-hour tramp, that duty, even outside the station on the surface of the asteroid where there's no gravity to speak of. We, in the recreation room, off duty, could tell by the sound of their voices as the inner port sucked open and the clanging clash of them removing their spacesuits came echoing to us along the metal corridor, that the Kid had been needling Clay through the whole tour.

'Another day,' came the Kid's voice, 'another fifty credits. And how's the piggy bank coming along, Clay?'

There was a slight pause, and I could see Clay carefully controlling his features and his voice. Then his pleasant baritone, softened by the burr of his Tarsusian accent, came smoothly to us.

'Like a gentleman, Kid,' he answered. 'He never overeats and so he runs no danger of indigestion.'

It was a neat answer, based on the fact that the Kid's own service account was swollen with his winnings from the rest of the crew. But the Kid was too thick-skinned for rapier thrusts. He laughed; and they finished removing their equipment and came on into the recreation room.

They made a striking picture as they entered, for they were enough alike to be brothers – although father and son would have been a more likely relationship, considering the difference in their ages. Both were tall, dark, wide-shouldered men with lean faces, but experience had weathered the softer lines from Clay's face and drawn thin parentheses about the corners of his mouth. There were other differences, too; but you could see in the Kid the youth that Clay had been, and in Clay the man that the Kid would someday be.

'Hi, Clay,' I said.

'Hello, Mort,' he said, sitting down beside me.

'Hi, Mort,' said the Kid.

I ignored him; and for a moment he tensed. I could see the anger flame up in the ebony depths of his black pupils under the heavy eyebrows. He was a big man; but I come from the Dorsai Planets and a Dorsai man fights to the death, if he fights at all. And, in consequence, among ourselves, we of Dorsai are a polite people.

But politeness was wasted on the Kid – as was Clay's delicate irony. With men like the Kid, you have to use a club.

We were in bad shape. The twenty of us at Frontier Station 563, on the periphery of the human area just beyond Sirius, had gone sour, and half the men had applications in for transfer. The trouble between Clay and the Kid was splitting the station wide open.

We were all in the Frontier Service for money; that was the root of the trouble. Fifty credits a day is good pay – but you have to sign up for a ten-year hitch. You can buy yourself out – but that costs a hundred thousand. Figure it out for yourself. Nearly six years if you saved every penny you got. So most go in with the idea of staying the full decade.

That was Clay's idea. He had gambled most of his life away. He had won and lost several fortunes. Now he was getting old and tired, and he wanted to go back – to Lulungomeena, on the little planet of Tarsus, which was the place he had come from as a young man.

But he was through with gambling. He said money made that way never stuck, but ran away again like quicksilver. So he drew his pay and banked it.

But the Kid was out for a killing. Four years of play with the rest of the crew had given him more than enough to buy his way out and leave him a nice stake. And perhaps he would have done just that, if it hadn't been that the Service account of Clay's drew him like an El Dorado. He could not go off and leave it. So he stayed with the outfit, riding the older man unmercifully.

He harped continually on two themes. He pretended to disbelieve that Clay had ever been a gambler; and he derided Lulungomeena, Clay's birthplace: the older man's goal and dream, and the one thing he could be drawn in to talk about. For, to Clay, Lulungomeena was beautiful, the most wonderful spot in the Universe; and with an old man's sick longing for home, he could not help saying so.

'Mort,' said the Kid, ignoring the rebuff and sitting down beside us, 'what's a Hixabrod like?'

My club had not worked so well, after all. Perhaps I, too, was slipping. Next to Clay, I was the oldest man on the crew, which was why we were close friends. I scowled at the Kid.

'Why?' I asked.

'We're having one for a visitor,' he said.

Immediately, all talk around the recreation room ceased, and all attention was focused on the Kid. All aliens had to clear through a station like ours when they crossed the frontier from one of the other great galactic power groups into human territory. But isolated as Station 563 was, it was seldom an alien came our way, and when one did, it was an occasion.

Even Clay succumbed to the general interest. 'I didn't know that,' he said. 'How'd you find out?'

'The notice came in over the receiver when you were down checking the atmosphere plant,' answered the Kid with a careless wave of his hand. 'I'd already filed it when you came up. What'll he be like, Mort?'

I had knocked around more than any of them – even Clay. This was my second stretch in the Service. I remembered back about twenty years, to the Denebian Trouble.

'Stiff as a poker,' I said. 'Proud as Lucifer, honest as sunlight, and tight as a camel on his way through the eye of a needle. Sort of a humanoid, but with a face like a collie dog. You know the Hixabrodian reputation, don't you?'

Somebody at the back of the crowd said no, although they may have been doing it just to humor me. Like Clay with his Lulungomeena, old age was making me garrulous.

'They're the first and only mercenary ambassadors in the known Universe,' I said. 'A Hixabrod can be hired, but he can't be influenced, bribed or forced to come up with anything but the cold truth – and, brother, it's cold the way a Hixabrod serves it up to you. That's why they're so much in demand. If any kind of political dispute comes up, from planetary to interalien power-group levels, both sides have to hire a Hixabrod to represent them in the discussions. That way they know the other side is being honest with them. The opposing Hixabrod is a living guarantee of that.'

'He sounds good,' said the Kid. 'What say we get together and throw him a good dinner during his twenty-four-hour stopover?'

'You won't get much in the way of thanks from him,' I grunted. 'They aren't built that way.'

'Let's do it anyway,' said the Kid. 'Be a little excitement for a change.'

A murmur of approval ran through the room. I was outvoted. Even Clay liked the idea.

'Hixabrods eat what we eat, don't they?' asked the Kid, making plans. 'Okay, then, soups, salad, meats, champagne and brandy – ' he ran on, ticking the items off on his fingers. For a moment, his enthusiasm had us all with him. But then, just at the end, he couldn't resist getting in one more dig at Clay.

'Oh, yes,' he finished, 'and for entertainment, you can tell him about Lulungomeena, Clay.'

Clay winced – not obviously, but we all saw a shadow cross his face. Lulungomeena on Tarsus, his birthplace, held the same sort of obsession for him that his Service account held for the Kid; but he could not help being aware that he was prone to let his tongue run away on the subject of its beauty. For it was where he belonged, in the stomach-twisting, throat-aching way that sometimes only talk can relieve.

I was a Dorsai man and older than the rest. I understood. No one should make fun of the bond tying a man to his home world. It is as real as it is intangible. And to joke about it is cruel.

But the Kid was too young to know that yet. He was fresh from Earth – Earth, where none of the rest of us had been, yet which, hundreds of years before, had been the origin of us all. He was eager and strong and contemptuous of emotion. He saw, as the rest of us recognized also, that Clay's tendency to let his talk wander ever to the wonder of Lulungomeena was the first slight crack in what had once been a man of unflawed steel. It was the first creeping decay of age.

But, unlike the rest of us, who hid our boredom out of sympathy, the Kid saw here a chance to break Clay and his resolution to do no more gambling. So he struck out constantly at this one spot so deeply vital that Clay's self-possession was no defense.

Now, at this last blow, the little fires of anger gathered in the older man's eyes.

'That's enough,' he said harshly. 'Leave Lulungomeena out of the discussion.'

'I'm willing to,' said the Kid. 'But somehow you keep reminding me of it. That and the story that you once were a gambler. If you won't prove the last one, how can you expect me to believe all you say about the first?'

The veins stood out on Clay's forehead, but he controlled himself.

'I've told you a thousand times,' he said between his teeth. 'Money made by gambling doesn't stick. You'll find that out for yourself one of these days.'

'Words,' said the Kid airily. 'Only words.'

For a second, Clay stood staring whitely at him, not even breathing. I don't know if the Kid realized his danger or cared, but I didn't breathe, either, until Clay's chest expanded, and he turned abruptly and walked out of the recreation room. We heard his bootsteps die away down the corridor toward his room in the dormitory section.

Later, I braced the Kid about it. It was his second-shift

time, when most of the men in the recreation room had to go on duty. I ran the Kid to the ground in the galley where he was fixing himself a sandwich. He looked up, a little startled, more than a little on the defensive, as I came in.

'Oh, hi, Mort,' he said with a pretty good imitation of casualness. 'What's up?'

'You,' I told him. 'Are you looking for a fight with Clay?'

'No,' he drawled with his mouth full. 'I wouldn't exactly say that.'

'Well, that's what you're liable to get.'

'Look, Mort,' he said, and then paused until he had swallowed. 'Don't you think Clay's old enough to look after himself?'

I felt a slight and not unpleasant shiver run down between my shoulder blades and my eyes began to grow hot. It was my Dorsai blood again. It must have showed on my face, for the Kid, who had been sitting negligently on one edge of the galley table, got up in a hurry.

'Hold on, Mort,' he said. 'Nothing personal.'

I fought the old feeling down and said as calmly as I could, 'I just dropped by to tell you something. Clay has been around a lot longer than you have. I'd advise you to lay off him.'

'Afraid he'll get hurt?'

'No,' I answered. 'I'm afraid you will.'

The Kid snorted with sudden laughter, half choking on his sandwich. 'Now I get it. You think I'm too young to take care of myself.'

'Something like that, but not the way you think. I want to tell you something about yourself, and you don't have to say whether I'm right or wrong – you'll let me know without words.'

'Hold it,' he said, turning red. 'I didn't come out here to get psyched.'

'You'll get it just the same. And it's not for you only – it's for all of us, because men thrown together as closely as we are choose up sides whenever there's conflict, and that's as dangerous for the rest of us as it is for you.'

'Then the rest of you can stay out of it.'

'We can't,' I said. 'What affects one of us affects us all. Now I'll tell you what you're doing. You came out here expecting to find glamour and excitement. You found monotony and boredom instead, not realizing that that's what space is like almost all the time.'

He picked up his coffee container. 'And now you'll say I'm trying to create my own excitement at Clay's expense. Isn't that the standard line?'

'I wouldn't know; I'm not going to use it, because that's not how I see what you're doing. Clay is adult enough to stand the monotony and boredom if they'll get him what he wants. He's also learned how to live with others and with himself. He doesn't have to prove himself by beating down somebody either half or twice his age.'

He took a drink and set the container down on the table. 'And I do?'

'All youngsters do. It's their way of experimenting with their potentialities and relationships with other people. When they find that out, they can give it up – they're mature then – although some never do. I think you will, eventually. The sooner you stop doing it here, though, the better it'll be for you and us.'

'And if I don't?' he challenged.

'This isn't college back on Earth or some other nice, safe home planet, where hazing can be a nuisance, but where it's possible to escape it by going somewhere else. There isn't any "somewhere else" there. Unless the one doing the hazing sees how reckless and dangerous it is, the one getting hazed takes it as long as he can – and then something happens.'

'So it's Clay you're really worried about, after all.'

'Look, get it through your skull. Clay's a man, and he's been through worse than this before. You haven't. If anybody's going to get hurt, it'll be you.'

He laughed and headed for the corridor door. He was still laughing as it slammed behind him. I let him go. There's no use pushing a bluff after it's failed to work.

The next day, the Hixabrod came. His name was Dor Lassos. He was typical of his race, taller than the tallest of us by half a head, with a light green skin and that impassive Hixabrodian canine face.

I missed his actual arrival, being up in the observation tower checking meteor paths. The station itself was well protected, but some of the ships coming in from time to time could have gotten in trouble with a few of the larger ones that slipped by us at intervals in that particular sector. When I did get free, Dor Lassos had already been assigned to his quarters and the time of official welcoming was over.

I went down to see him anyhow on the off-chance that we had mutual acquaintances either among his race or mine. Both of our peoples are few enough in number, God knows, so the possibility wasn't too far-fetched. And, like Clay, I yearned for anything connected with my home.

'*Wer velt d'hatchen, Hixabrod –* ' I began, walking into his apartment – and stopped short.

The Kid was there. He looked at me with an odd expression on his face.

'Do you speak Hixabrodian?' he asked incredulously.

I nodded. I had learned it on extended duty during the Denebian Trouble. Then I remembered my manners and turned back to the Hixabrod; but he was already started on his answer.

'*En gles Ter, I tu, Dorsaiven,*' returned the collie face, expressionlessly. '*Da Tr'amgen lang. Met zurres nebent?*'

'*Em getluc. Me mi Dorsai fene. Nono ne – ves luc Les Lassos?*'

He shook his head.

Well, it had been a shot in the dark anyway. There was only the faintest chance that he had known our old interpreter at the time of the Denebian Trouble. The Hixabrods have no family system of nomenclature. They take their names from the names of older Hixabrods they admire or like. I bowed politely to him and left.

It was not until later that it occurred to me to wonder what in the Universe the Kid could find to talk about with a Hixabrod.

I actually was worried about Clay. Since my bluff with the Kid had failed, I thought I might perhaps try with Clay himself. At first I waited for an opportune moment to turn up; but following the last argument with the Kid, he'd been sticking to his quarters. I finally scrapped the casual approach and went to see him.

I found him in his quarters, reading. It was a little shocking to find that tall, still athletic figure in a dressing gown like an old man, eyes shaded by the lean fingers of one long hand, poring over the little glow of a scanner with the lines unreeling before his eyes. But he looked up as I came in, and the smile on his face was the smile I had grown familiar with over four years of close living together.

'What's that?' I asked, nodding at the book scanner.

He set it down, and the little light went out, the lines stopped unreeling.

'A bad novel,' he said, smiling, 'by a poor author. But they're both Tarsusian.'

I took the chair he had indicated. 'Mind if I speak straight out, Clay?'

'Go ahead,' he invited.

'The Kid,' I said bluntly. 'And you. The two of you can't go on this way.'

'Well, old fire-eater,' answered Clay lightly, 'what've you got to suggest?'

'Two things. And I want you to think both of them over carefully before answering. First, we see if we can't get up a nine-tenths majority here in the station and petition him out as incompatible.'

Clay slowly shook his head. 'We can't do that, Mort.'

'I think I can get the signatures if I ask it,' I said. 'Everybody's pretty tired of him. . . . They'd come across.'

'It's not that, and you know it,' said Clay. 'Transfer by petition isn't supposed to be prejudicial, but you and I know it is. He'd be switched to some hard-case station, get in worse trouble there, and end up in a penal post generally shot to hell. He'd know who to blame for it, and he'd hate us for the rest of his life.'

'What of it? Let him hate us.'

'I'm a Tarsusian. It'd bother me, and I couldn't do it.'

'All right,' I said. 'Dropping that, then, you've got nearly seven years in, total, and half the funds you need to buy out. I've got nearly enough saved, in spite of myself, to make up the rest. In addition, for your retirement, I'll sign over to you my pay for the three years I've got left. Take that and get out of the Service. It isn't what you figured on having, but half a loaf . . . '

'And how about your home-going?' he asked.

'Look at me.'

He looked; and I knew what he was seeing – the broken nose, the scars, the lined face – the Dorsai face.

'I'll never go home,' I said.

He sat looking at me for a long moment more, and I fancied I saw a little burn deep in back of his eyes. But then the light went out, and I knew that I'd lost with him, too.

'Maybe not,' he said quietly. 'But I'm not going to be the one that keeps you from it.'

I left him to his book.

Shifts are supposed to run continuously, with someone on duty all the time. However, for special occasions, like this dinner we had arranged for the Hixabrod, it was possible, by getting work done ahead of time and picking the one four-hour stretch during the twenty-four when there were no messages or ships due in, to assemble everybody in the station on an off-duty basis.

So we were all there that evening, in the recreation room, which had been cleared and set up with a long table for the dinner. We finished our cocktails, sat down at the table, and the meal began.

As it will, the talk during the various courses turned to things outside the narrow limits of our present lives. Remembrances of places visited, memories of an earlier life, and the comparison of experiences, some of them pretty weird, were the materials of which our table talk was built.

Unconsciously, all of us were trying to draw the Hixabrod out. But he sat in his place at the head of the table between Clay and myself, with the Kid a little farther down, preserving a frosty silence until the dessert had been disposed of and the subject of Media unexpectedly came up.

'Media,' said the Kid. 'I've heard of Media. It's a little planet, but it's supposed to have everything from soup to nuts on it in the way of life. There's one little life-form there that's claimed to contain something of value to every metabolism. It's called – let me see now – it's called –'

'It is called *nygti*,' supplied Dor Lassos, suddenly, in a metallic voice. 'A small quadruped with a highly complex nervous system and a good deal of fatty tissue. I visited the planet over eighty years ago, before it was actually opened up to general travel. The food stores spoiled, and we had the opportunity of testing out the theory that it will provide sustenance for almost any kind of known intelligent being.'

He stopped.

'Well?' demanded the Kid. 'Since you're here to tell the story, I assume the animal kept you alive.'

'I and the humans aboard the ship found the *nygti* quite nourishing,' said Dor Lassos. 'Unfortunately, we had several Micrushni from Polaris also aboard.'

'And those?' asked someone.

'A highly developed but inelastic life-form,' said Dor Lassos, sipping from his brandy glass. 'They went into convulsions and died.'

I had had some experience with Hixabrodian ways, and I knew that it was not sadism but a complete detachment that had prompted this little anecdote. But I could see a wave of distaste ripple down the room. No life-form is so universally well liked as the Micrushni, a delicate iridescent jellyfishlike race with a bent toward poetry and philosophy.

The men at the table drew away almost visibly from Dor Lassos. But that affected him no more than if they had applauded loudly. Only in very limited ways are the Hixabrod capable of empathy where other races are concerned.

'That's too bad,' said Clay slowly. 'I have always liked the Micrushni.' He had been drinking somewhat heavily, and the seemingly innocuous statement came out like a half-challenge. Dor Lassos' cold brown eyes turned and rested on him. Whatever he saw, whatever conclusions he came to, however, were hidden behind his emotionless face.

'In general,' he said flatly, 'a truthful race.'

That was the closest a Hixabrod could come to praise, and I expected the matter to drop there. But the Kid spoke up again.

'Not like us humans,' he said. 'Eh, Dor Lassos?'

I glared at him from behind Dor Lassos' head. But he went recklessly on.

'I said, "Not like us humans, eh?" ' he repeated loudly. The Kid had also apparently been drinking freely, and his voice grated on the sudden silence of the room.

'The human race varies,' stated the Hixabrod emotionlessly. 'You have some individuals who approach truth. Otherwise, the human race is not notably truthful.'

It was a typical, deadly accurate Hixabrodian response. Dor Lassos would have answered in the same words if his throat was to have been cut for them the minute they left his mouth. Again, it should have shut the Kid up, and again it apparently failed.

'Ah, yes,' said the Kid. 'Some approach truth, but in general we are untruthful. But you see, Dor Lassos, a certain amount of human humor is associated with lies. Some of us tell lies just for fun.'

Dor Lassos drank from his brandy glass and said nothing.

'Of course,' the Kid went on, 'sometimes a human thinks he's being funny with his lies when he isn't. Some lies are just boring, particularly when you're forced to hear them over and over again. But on the other hand, there are some champion liars who are so good that even you would find their untruths humorous.'

Clay sat upright suddenly, and the sudden start of his movement sent his brandy slopping out over the rim of his glass and onto the white tablecloth. He stared at the Kid.

I looked at them all – at Clay, at the Kid, and at Dor Lassos – and an ugly premonition began to form in my brain.

'I do not believe I should,' said Dor Lassos.

'Ah, but you should listen to a real expert,' said the Kid feverishly, 'when he has a good subject to work on. Now, for example, take the matter of home worlds. What is your home world, Hixa, like?'

I had heard enough and more than enough to confirm the suspicion forming within me. Without drawing any undue attention to myself, I rose and left the room.

The alien made a dry sound in his throat, and his voice followed me as I went swiftly down the empty corridor.

'It is very beautiful,' he said in his adding-machine tones. 'Hixa has a diameter of thirty-eight thousand universal meters. It possesses twenty-three great mountain ranges and seventeen large bodies of salt water. . . . '

The sound of his voice died away, and I left it behind me.

I went directly through the empty corridors and up the ladder to the communications shack. I went in the door without pausing, without – in neglect of all duty rules – glancing at the automatic printer to see if any fresh message out of routine had arrived, without bothering to check the transmitter to see that it was keyed into the automatic location signal for approaching spacecraft.

All this I ignored and went directly to the file where the incoming messages are kept.

I flicked the tab and went back to the file of two days previous, skimming through the thick sheaf of transcripts under that dateline. And there, beneath the heading 'Notices of Arrivals', I found it, the message announcing the coming of Dor Lassos. I ran my finger down past the statistics on our guest to the line of type that told me where the Hixabrod's last stop had been.

Tarsus.

Clay was my friend. And there is a limit to what a man can take without breaking. On a wall of the communications shack was a roster of the men at our station. I drew the Dorsai sign against the name of William Peterborough, and checked my gun out of the arms locker.

I examined the magazine. It was loaded. I replaced the magazine, put the gun inside my jacket, and went back to the dinner.

Dor Lassos was still talking.

' . . . The flora and the fauna are maintained in such excellent natural balance that no local surplus has exceeded one per cent of the normal population for any species in the last sixty thousand years. Life on Hixa is regular and predictable. The weather is controlled within the greatest limits of feasibility.'

As I took my seat, the machine voice of the Hixabrod hesitated for just a moment, then gathered itself, and went on: 'One day I shall return there.'

'A pretty picture,' said the Kid. He was leaning forward over the table now, his eyes bright, his teeth bared in a smile. 'A very attractive home world. But I regret to inform you, Dor Lassos, that I've been given to understand that it pales into insignificance when compared to one other spot in the Galaxy.'

The Hixabrod are warriors, too. Dor Lassos' features remained expressionless, but his voice deepened and rang through the room.

'Your planet?'

'I wish it were,' returned the Kid with the same wolfish smile. 'I wish I could lay claim to it. But this place is so wonderful that I doubt if I would be allowed there. In fact,' the Kid went on, 'I have never seen it. But I have been hearing about it for some years now. And either it is the most wonderful place in the Universe, or else the man who has been telling about it – '

I pushed my chair back and started to rise, but Clay's hand clamped on my arm and held me down.

'You were saying –' he said to the Kid, who had been inter-rupted by my movement.

'The man who has been telling me about it,' said the Kid, deliberately, 'is one of those champion liars I was telling Dor Lassos about.'

Once more I tried to get to my feet, but Clay was there before me. Tall and stiff, he stood at the end of the table.

'My right –' he said out of the corner of his mouth to me.

Slowly and with meaning, he picked up his brandy glass and threw the glass straight into the Kid's face. It bounced on the table in front of him and sent brandy flying over the front of the Kid's immaculate dress uniform.

'Get your gun!' ordered Clay.

Now the Kid was on his feet. In spite of the fact that I knew he had planned this, emotion had gotten the better of him at the end. His face was white with rage. He leaned on the edge of the table and fought with himself to carry it through as he had originally intended.

'Why guns?' he said. His voice was thick with restraint, as he struggled to control himself.

'You called me a liar.'

'Will guns tell me if you are?' The Kid straightened up, breathing more easily, and his laugh was harsh in the room. 'Why use guns when it's possible to prove the thing one way or another with complete certainty?' His gaze swept the room and came back to Clay.

'For years now you've been telling me all sorts of things,' he said. 'But two things you've told me more than all the rest. One was that you used to be a gambler. The other was that Lulungomeena – your precious Lulungomeena on Tarsus – was the most wonderful place in the Universe. Is either one of those the truth?'

Clay's breath came thick and slow.

'They're both the truth,' he said, fighting to keep his voice steady.

'Will you back that up?'

'With my life!'

'Ah,' said the Kid mockingly, holding up his forefinger, 'but I'm not asking you to back those statements up with your life –

but with that neat little hoard you've been accumulating these past years. You claimed you're a gambler. Will you bet that those statements are true?'

Now, for the first time, Clay seemed to see the trap.

'Bet with me,' invited the Kid, almost lightly. 'That will prove the first statement.'

'And what about the second?' demanded Clay.

'Why' – the Kid gestured with his hand toward Dor Lassos – 'what further judge do we need? We have here at our table a Hixabrod.' Half turning to the alien, the Kid made him a little bow. 'Let him say whether your second statement is true or not.'

Once more I tried to rise from my seat, and again Clay's hand shoved me down. He turned to Dor Lassos.

'Do you think you could judge such a point, sir?' he asked.

The brown inhuman eyes met his and held for a long moment.

'I have just come from Tarsus,' said the Hixabrod. 'I was there as a member of the Galactic Survey Team, mapping the planet. It was my duty to certify to the truth of the map.'

The choice was no choice. Clay stood staring at the Hixabrod as the room waited for his answer. Rage burning within me, I looked down the table for a sign in the faces of the others that this thing might be stopped. But where I expected to see sympathy, there was nothing. Instead, there was blankness, or cynicism, or even the wet-lipped interest of men who like their excitement written in blood or tears.

And I realized with a sudden sinking of hopes that I stood alone, after all, as Clay's friend. In my own approaching age and garrulity I had not minded his talk of Lulungomeena, hour on repetitive hour. But these others had grown weary of it. Where I saw tragedy, they saw only retribution coming to a lying bore.

And what Clay saw was what I saw. His eyes went dark and cold.

'How much will you bet?' he asked.

'All I've got,' responded the Kid, leaning forward eagerly. 'Enough and more than enough to match that bank roll of yours. The equivalent of eight years' pay.'

Stiffly, without a word, Clay produced his savings book and a voucher pad. He wrote out a voucher for the whole amount and laid book and voucher on the table before Dor Lassos. The Kid, who had obviously come prepared, did the same, adding a thick pile of cash from his gambling of recent weeks.

'That's all of it?' asked Clay.

'All of it,' said the Kid.

Clay nodded and stepped back.

'Go ahead,' he said.

The Kid turned toward the alien.

'Dor Lassos,' he said. 'We appreciate your cooperation in this matter.'

'I am glad to hear it,' responded the Hixabrod, 'since my cooperation will cost the winner of the bet a thousand credits.'

The abrupt injection of this commercial note threw the Kid momentarily off stride. I, alone in the room, who knew the Hixabrod people, had expected it. But the rest had not, and it struck a sour note, which reflected back on the Kid. Up until now, the bet had seemed to most of the others like a cruel but at least honest game, concerning ourselves only. Suddenly it had become a little like hiring a paid bully to beat up a station-mate.

But it was too late now to stop, the bet had been made. Nevertheless, there were murmurs from different parts of the room.

The Kid hurried on, fearful of the interruption. Clay's savings were on his mind.

'You were a member of the mapping survey team?' he asked Dor Lassos.

'I was,' said the Hixabrod.

'Then you know the planet?'

'I do.'

'You know its geography?' insisted the Kid.

'I do not repeat myself.' The eyes of the Hixabrod were chill and withdrawn, almost a little baleful, as they met those of the Kid.

'What kind of a planet is it?' The Kid licked his lips. He was beginning to recover his usual self-assurance. 'Is it a large planet?'

'No.'

'Is Tarsus a rich planet?'

'No.'

'Is it a pretty planet?'

'I did not find it so.'

'*Get to the point!*' snapped Clay with strained harshness.

The Kid glanced at him, savoring this moment. He turned back to the Hixabrod.

'Very well, Dor Lassos,' he said, 'we get to the meat of the matter. Have you ever heard of Lulungomeena?'

'Yes.'

'Have you ever been to Lulungomeena?'

'I have.'

'And do you truthfully' – for the first time, a fierce and burning anger flashed momentarily in the eyes of the Hixabrod; the insult the Kid had just unthinkingly given Dor Lassos was a deadly one – '*truthfully* say that in your considered opinion Lulungomeena is the most wonderful place in the Universe?'

Dor Lassos turned his gaze away from him and let it wander over the rest of the room. Now, at last, his contempt for all there was plain to be read on his face.

'*Yes, it is,*' said Dor Lassos.

He rose to his feet at the head of the stunned group around the table. From the pile of cash he extracted a thousand credits, then passed the remainder, along with the two account books and the vouchers, to Clay. Then he took one step toward the Kid.

He halted before him and offered his hands to the man – palms up, the tips of his fingers a scant couple of inches short of the Kid's face.

'My hands are clean,' he said.

His fingers arced; and, suddenly, as we watched, stubby, gleaming claws shot smoothly from those fingertips to tremble lightly against the skin of the Kid's face.

'Do you doubt the truthfulness of a Hixabrod?' his robot voice asked.

The Kid's face was white, and his cheeks hollowed in fear. The needle points of the claws were very close to his eyes. He swallowed once.

'No – ' he whispered.

The claws retracted. The hands returned to their owner's sides. Once more completely withdrawn and impersonal, Dor Lassos turned and bowed to us all.

'My appreciation of your courtesy,' he said, the metallic

tones of his voice loud in the silence.

Then he turned and, marching like a metronome, disappeared through the doorway of the recreation room and off in the direction of his quarters.

'And so we part,' said Clay Harbank as we shook hands. 'I hope you find the Dorsai Planets as welcome as I intend to find Lulungomeena.'

I grumbled a little. 'That was plain damn foolishness. You didn't have to buy me out as well.'

'There were more than enough credits for the both of us,' said Clay.

It was a month after the bet and the two of us were standing in the Deneb One spaceport. For miles in every direction, the great echoing building of this central terminal stretched around us. In ten minutes I was due to board my ship for the Dorsai Planets. Clay himself still had several days to wait before one of the infrequent ships to Tarsus would be ready to leave.

'The bet itself was damn foolishness,' I went on, determined to find something to complain about. We Dorsai do not enjoy these moments of emotion. But a Dorsai is a Dorsai. I am not apologizing.

'No foolishness,' said Clay. For a moment a shadow crossed his face. 'You forget that a real gambler bets only on a sure thing. When I looked into the Hixabrod's eyes, I was sure.'

'How can you say "a sure thing"?'

'The Hixabrod loved his home,' Clay said.

I stared at him, astounded. 'But you weren't betting on Hixa. Of course he would prefer Hixa to any other place in the Universe. But you were betting on Tarsus – on Lulungomeena – remember?'

The shadow was back for a moment on Clay's face. 'The bet was certain. I feel a little guilty about the Kid, but I warned him that gambling money never stuck. Besides, he's young, and I'm getting old. I couldn't afford to lose.'

'Will you come down out of the clouds,' I demanded, 'and explain this thing? Why was the bet certain? What was the trick, if there was one?'

'The trick?' repeated Clay. He smiled at me. 'The trick was that the Hixabrod could not be otherwise than truthful. It was all in the name of my birthplace – Lulungomeena.'

He looked at my puzzled face and put a hand on my shoulder.

'You see, Mort,' he said quietly, 'it was the name that fooled everybody. Lulungomeena stands for something in my language. But not for any city or town or village. Everybody on Tarsus has his own Lulungomeena. Everybody in the Universe has.'

'How do you figure that, Clay?'

'It's a word,' he explained. 'A word in the Tarsusian language. It means "home".'

The Dance of the Changer and the Three

TERRY CARR

One of the most difficult challenges a science-fiction writer can set for himself is the depiction of a wholly alien culture. The problem is to create a way of life and a consciousness utterly different from anything found on Earth, and yet to depict it in a manner that an Earth-born reader can comprehend. Students of philosophy maintain that such a goal is probably impossible to fulfil – that every writer, even the most imaginative, simply rearranges and re-combines various aspects of the known in his attempts to invent the unknown. Maybe so; nevertheless, it seems to me that Terry Carr has come extraordinarily close to achieving the impossible in this haunting narrative of strange rites in a distant galaxy.

This all happened ages ago, out of the depths of space beyond Darkedge, where galaxies lumber ponderously through the black like so many silent bright rhinoceroses. It was so long ago that when the light from Loarr's galaxy finally reached Earth, after millions of light-years, there was no one here to see it except a few things in the oceans that were too mindlessly busy with their monotonous single-celled reactions to notice.

Yet, so long ago as it was, the present-day Loarra still remember this story and retell it in complex, shifting wave-dances every time one of the newly changed asks for it. The wave-dances wouldn't mean much to you if you saw them, nor I suppose would the story itself if I were to tell it just as it happened. So consider this a translation, and don't bother yourself that when I say 'water' I don't mean our hydrogen-oxygen compound, or that there's no 'sky' as such on Loarr, or for that matter that the Loarra weren't – aren't – creatures that 'think' or 'feel' in quite the way we understand. In fact, you could take this as a piece of pure fiction, because there are damned few real facts in it – but I know better (or worse), because I know how true it is. And that has a lot to do with why I'm back here on Earth, with forty-two friends and co-workers left dead on Loarr. They never had a chance.

There was a Changer who had spent three life cycles planning a particular cycleclimax and who had come to the moment of action. He wasn't really named Minnearo, but I'll call him that because it's the closest thing I can write to approximate the tone, emotional matrix, and association that were all wrapped up in his designation.

When he came to his decision, he turned away from the crag on which he'd been standing overlooking the Loarran ocean, and went quickly to the personality-homes of three of his best friends. To the first friend, Asterrea, he said, 'I am going to commit suicide,' wave-dancing this message in his best festive tone.

His friend laughed, as Minnearo had hoped, but only for a short time. Then he turned away and left Minnearo alone, because there had already been several suicides lately, and it was wearing a little thin.

To his second friend, Minnearo gave a pledge-salute, going through all sixty sequences with exaggerated care, and wave-danced, 'Tomorrow I shall immerse my body in the ocean, if anyone will watch.'

His second friend, Fless, smiled tolerantly and told him he would come and see the performance.

To his third friend, with many excited leapings and bound-ings, Minnearo described what he imagined would happen to him after he had gone under the lapping waters of the ocean. The dance he went through to give this description was intricate and even imaginative, because Minnearo had spent most of that third life cycle working it out in his mind. It used motion and color and sound and another sense something like smell, all to communicate descriptions of falling, impact with the water, and then the quick dissolution and blending in the currents of the ocean, the dimming and loss of awareness, then darkness, and finally the awakening, the completion of the change. Minnearo had a rather romantic turn of mind, so he imagined himself recoalescing around the life-mote of one of Loarr's greatest heroes, Krollim, and forming on Krollim's

137

old pattern. And he even ended the dance with suggestions of glory and imitation of himself by others, which was definitely presumptuous. But the friend for whom the dance was given did nod approvingly at several points.

'If it turns out to be half what you anticipate,' said this friend, Pur, 'then I envy you. But you never know.'

'I guess not,' Minnearo said, rather morosely. And he hesitated before leaving, for Pur was what I suppose I'd better call female, and Minnearo had rather hoped that she would join him in the ocean jump. But if she thought of it, she gave no sign, merely gazing at Minnearo calmly, waiting for him to go; so finally he did.

And at the appropriate time, with his friend Fless watching him from the edge of the cliff, Minnearo did his final wave-dance as Minnearo – rather excited and ill-coordinated, but that was understandable in the circumstances – and then performed his approach to the edge, leaped and tumbled downward through the air, making fully two dozen turns this way and that before he hit the water.

Fless hurried back and described the suicide to Asterrea and Pur who laughed and applauded in most of the right places, so on the whole it was a success. Then the three of them sat down and began plotting Minnearo's revenge.

– All right, I know a lot of this doesn't make sense. Maybe that's because I'm trying to tell you about the Loarra in human terms, which is a mistake with creatures as alien as they are. Actually, the Loarra are almost wholly an energy life-form, their consciousnesses coalescing in each life cycle around a spatial center which they call a life-mote, so that, if you could see the patterns of energy they form (as I have, using a sense filter our expedition developed for that purpose), they'd look rather like a spiral nebula sometimes, or other times like iron filings gathering around a magnet, or maybe like a half-melted snowflake. (That's probably what Minnearo looked like on that day, because it's the suicides and the aged who look like that.) Their forms keep shifting, of course, but each individual usually keeps close to one pattern.

Loarr itself is a gigantic gaseous planet with an orbit so close to its primary that its year has to be only about thirty-seven Earthstandard Days long. (In Earthsystem, the orbit would be considerably inside that of Venus.) There's a solid core to the planet, and a lot of hard outcroppings like islands, but most of the surface is in a molten or gaseous state, swirling and bubbling and howling with winds and storms. It's not a very inviting planet if you're anything like a human being, but it does have one thing that brought it to Unicentral's attention: mining.

Do you have any idea what mining is like on a planet where most metals are fluid from the heat and/or pressure? Most people haven't heard much about this, because it isn't a situation we encounter often, but it was there on Loarr, and it was very, very interesting. Because our analyses showed some elements that had been until then only computer-theory – elements that were supposed to exist only in the hearts of suns, for one thing. And if we could get hold of some of them . . . Well, you see what I mean. The mining possibilities were very interesting indeed.

Of course, it would take half the wealth of Earthsystem to outfit a full-scale expedition there. But Unicentral hummed for two-point-eight seconds and then issued detailed instructions on just how it was all to be arranged. So there we went.

And there I was, a Standard Year later (five Standard Years ago), sitting inside a mountain of artificial Earth welded onto one of Loarr's 'islands' and wondering what the hell I was doing there. Because I'm not a mining engineer, not a physicist or comp-technician or, in fact, much of anything that requires technical training. I'm a public-relations man; and there was just no reason for me to have been assigned to such a hellish, impossible, god-forsaken, inconceivable, and plain damned *unlivable* planet as Loarr.

But there was a reason, and it was the Loarra, of course. They lived ('lived') there, and they were intelligent, so we had to negotiate with them. Ergo: me.

So in the next several years, while I negotiated and we set up operations and I acted as a go-between, I learned a lot about them. Just enough to translate, however clumsily, the wave-dance of the Changer and the Three, which is their equivalent of a classic folk-hero myth (or would be if they had anything honestly equivalent to anything of ours).

To continue:

Fless was in favor of building a pact among the Three by which they would, each in turn and each with deliberate lack

139

of the appropriate salutes, commit suicide in exactly the same way Minnearo had. 'Thus we can kill this suicide,' Fless explained in excited waves through the air.

But Pur was more practical. 'Thus,' she corrected him, 'we would kill *only* this suicide. It is unimaginative, a thing to be done by rote, and Minnearo deserves more.'

Asterrea seemed undecided; he hopped about, sparking and disappearing and reappearing inches away in another color. They waited for him to comment, and finally he stabilized, stood still in the air, settled to the ground, and held himself firmly there. Then he said, in slow, careful movements, 'I'm not sure he deserves an original revenge. It wasn't a new suicide, after all. And who is to avenge us?' A single spark leaped from him. 'Who is to avenge us?' he repeated, this time with more pronounced motions.

'Perhaps,' said Pur slowly, 'we will need no revenge – if our act is great enough.'

The other two paused in their random wave-motions, considering this. Fless shifted from blue to green to a bright red which dimmed to yellow; Asterrea pulsed a deep ultraviolet.

'Everyone has always been avenged,' Fless said at last. 'What you suggest is meaningless.'

'But if we do something *great* enough,' Pur said; and now she began to radiate heat which drew the other two reluctantly toward her. 'Something which has never been done before, in *any* form. Something for which there can be no revenge, for it will be a *positive* thing – not a death-change, not a destruction or a disappearance or a forgetting, even a great one. A *positive* thing.'

Asterrea's ultraviolet grew darker, darker, until he seemed to be nothing more than a hole in the air. 'Dangerous, dangerous, dangerous,' he droned, moving torpidly back and forth. 'You know it's impossible to ask – we'd have to give up all our life cycles to come. Because a positive in the world . . . ' He blinked into darkness, and did not reappear for long seconds. When he did, he was perfectly still, pulsing weakly but gradually regaining strength.

Pur waited till his color and tone showed that consciousness had returned, then moved in a light wave-motion calculated to draw the other two back into calm, reasonable discourse. 'I've thought about this for six life cycles already,' she danced. 'I must be right – *no* one has worked on a problem for so long. A positive would *not* be dangerous, no matter what the three- and four-cycle theories say. It would be beneficial.' She paused, hanging orange in midair. 'And it would be *new*,' she said with a quick spiral. 'Oh, how *new*!'

And so, at length, they agreed to follow her plan. And it was briefly this: On a far island outcropping set in the deepest part of the Loarran ocean, where crashing, tearing storms whipped molten metal-compounds into blinding spray, there was a vortex of forces that was avoided by every Loarra on pain of inescapable and final death-change. The most ancient wave-dances of that ancient time said that the vortex had always been there, that the Loarra themselves had been born there or had escaped from there or had in some way cheated the laws that ruled there. Whatever the truth about that was, the vortex was an eater of energy, calling and catching from afar any Loarra or other beings who strayed within its influence. (For all the life on Loarr is energy-based, even the mindless, drifting foodbeasts – creatures of uniform dull color, no internal motion, no scent or tone, and absolutely no self-volition. Their place in the Loarran scheme of things is and was literally nothing more than that of food; even though there were countless food-beasts drifting in the air in most areas of the planet, the Loarra hardly ever noticed them. They ate them when they were hungry, and looked around them at any other time.)

'Then you want us to destroy the *vortex*?' cried Fless, dancing and dodging to right and left in agitation.

'Not *destroy*,' Pur said calmly. 'It will be a *life*-change, not a destruction.'

'Life-change?' said Asterrea faintly, wavering in the air.

And she said it again: '*Life*-change.' For the vortex had once created, or somehow allowed to be created, the Oldest of the Loarra, those many-cycles-ago beings who had combined and split, reacted and changed countless times to become the Loarra of this day. And if creation could happen at the vortex once, then it could happen again.

'But how?' asked Fless, trying now to be reasonable, dancing the question with precision and holding a steady green color as he did so.

'We will need help,' Pur said, and went on to explain that she had heard – from a windbird, a creature with little intelligence but perfect memory – that there was one of the Oldest still living his first life cycle in a personality-home somewhere near the vortex. In that most ancient time of the race, when suicide had been considered extreme as a means of cycle-change, this Oldest had made his change by a sort of negative suicide – he had frozen his cycle, so that his consciousness and form continued in a never-ending repetition of themselves, on and on while his friends changed and grew and learned as they ran through life cycle after life cycle, becoming different people with common memories, moving forward into the future by this method while he, the last Oldest, remained fixed at the beginning. He saw only the beginning, remembered only the beginning, understood only the beginning.

And for that reason his had been the most tragic of all Loarran changes (and the windbird had heard it rumored, in eight different ways, each of which it repeated word for word to Pur, that in the ages since that change more than a hundred hundred Loarra had attempted revenge for the Oldest, but always without success) and it had never been repeated, so that this Oldest was the only Oldest. And for that reason he was important to their quest, Pur explained.

With a perplexed growing and shrinking, brightening and dimming, Asterrea asked, 'But how can he live anywhere near the vortex and not be consumed by it?'

'That is a crucial part of what we must find out,' Pur said. And after the proper salutes and rituals, the Three set out to find the Oldest.

The wave-dance of the Changer and the Three traditionally at this point spends a great deal of time, in great splashes of color and bursts of light and subtly contrived clouds of darkness all interplaying with hops and swoops and blinking and dodging back and forth, to describe the scene as Pur, Fless, and Asterrea set off across that ancient molten sea. I've seen the dance countless times, and each viewing has seemed to bring me maddeningly closer to understanding the meaning that this has for the Loarra themselves. Lowering clouds flashing bursts of aimless, lifeless energy, a rumbling sea below, whose swirling depths pulled and tugged at the Three as they swept overhead, darting around each other in complex patterns like electrons playing cat's-cradle around an invisible nucleus. A droning of lamentation from the changers left behind on their rugged home island, and giggles from those who had recently changed. And the colors of the Three themselves: burning red Asterrea and glowing green Fless and steady, steady golden Pur. I see and hear them all, but I feel only a weird kind of alien beauty, not the grandeur, excitement, and awesomeness they have for the Loarra.

When the Three felt the vibrations and swirlings in the air that told them they were coming near to the vortex, they paused in their flight and hung in an inter-patterned motion-sequence above the dark, rolling sea, conversing only in short flickerings of color because they had to hold the pattern tightly in order to withstand the already strong attraction of the vortex.

'Somewhere near?' asked Asterrea, pulsing a quick green.

'Closer to the vortex, I think,' Pur said, chancing a sequence of reds and violets.

'Can we be sure?' asked Fless; but there was no answer from Pur, and he had expected none from Asterrea.

The ocean crashed and leaped; the air howled around them. And the vortex pulled at them.

Suddenly they felt their motion-sequence changing, against their wills, and for long moments all three were afraid that it was the vortex's attraction that was doing it. They moved in closer to each other, and whirled more quickly in a still more intricate pattern, but it did no good. Irresistibly they were drawn apart again, and at the same time the three of them were moved toward the vortex.

And then they felt the Oldest among them.

He had joined the motion-sequence; this must have been why they had felt the sequence changed and loosened – to make room for him. Whirling and blinking, the Oldest led them inward over the frightening sea, radiating warmth through the storm, and as they followed or were pulled along, they studied him in wonder.

He was hardly recognizable as one of them, this ancient Oldest. He was . . . not quite energy any longer. He was half matter, carrying the strange mass with awkward, aged grace, his outer edges almost rigid as they held the burden of his congealed center and carried it through the air. (Looking rather like a half-dissolved snowflake, yes, only dark and dismal, a snowflake weighted with coal dust.) And, for now at least, he was completely silent.

Only when he had brought the Three safely into the calm of his barren personality-home on a tiny rock jutting at an angle from the wash of the sea did he speak. There, inside a cone of quiet against which the ocean raged and fell back, the winds faltered and even the vortex's power was nullified, the Oldest said wearily, 'So you have come.' He spoke with a slow waving back and forth, augmented by only a dull red color.

To this the Three did not know what to say; but Pur finally hazarded, 'Have you been waiting for us?'

The Oldest pulsed a somewhat brighter red, once, twice. He paused. Then he said, 'I do not *wait* – there is nothing to wait *for*.' Again the pulse of a brighter red. 'One waits for the future. But there is no future, you know.'

'Not for him,' Pur said softly to her companions, and Fless and Asterrea sank wavering to the stone floor of the Oldest's home, where they rocked back and forth.

The Oldest sank with them, and when he touched down, he remained motionless. Pur drifted over the others, maintaining movement but unable to raise her color above a steady blue-green. She said to the Oldest, 'But you knew we would come.'

'Would come? *Would* come? Yes, and *did* come, and *have* come, and *are* come. It is today only, you know, for me. I will be the Oldest, when the others pass me by. I will never change, nor will my world.'

'But the others have already passed you by,' Fless said. 'We are many life cycles after you, Oldest – so many it is beyond the count of windbirds.'

The Oldest seemed to draw his material self into a more upright posture, forming his energy-flow carefully around it. To the red of his color he added a low hum with only the slightest quaver as he said, '*Nothing* is after me, here on Rock. When you come here, you come out of time, just as I have. So now you have always been here and will always be here, for as long as you are here.'

Asterrea sparked yellow suddenly and danced upward into the becalmed air. As Fless stared and Pur moved quickly to calm him, he drove himself again and again at the edge of the cone of quiet that was the Oldest's refuge. Each time he was thrown back, and each time he returned to dash himself once more against the edge of the storm, trying to penetrate back into it. He flashed and burned countless colors, and strange sound-frequencies filled the quiet, until at last, with Pur's stern direction and Fless's blank gaze upon him, he sank back wearily to the stone floor. 'A trap, a trap,' he pulsed. 'This is it, this is the vortex itself, we should have known, and we'll never get away.'

The Oldest had paid no attention to Asterrea's display. He said slowly, 'And it is because I am not in time that the vortex cannot touch me. And it is because I am out of time that I know what the vortex is, for I can remember myself born in it.'

Pur left Asterrea then, and came close to the Oldest. She hung above him, thinking with blue vibrations, then asked, 'Can you tell us how you were born? – what is creation? – how new things are made?' She paused a moment, and added, 'And what *is* the vortex?'

The Oldest seemed to lean forward, seemed tired. His color had deepened again to the darkest red, and the Three could clearly see every atom of matter within his energy-field, stark and hard. He said, 'So many questions to ask one question.' And he told them the answer to that question.

– And I can't tell you that answer, because I don't know it. No one knows it now, not even the present-day Loarra who are the Three after a thousand million billion life cycles. Because the Loarra really do become different ... different 'persons', when they pass from one cycle to another, and after that many changes, memory becomes meaningless. ('Try it sometime', one of the Loarra once wave-danced to me, and there was no indication that he thought this was a joke.)

Today, for instance, the Three themselves, a thousand million billion times removed from themselves but still, they maintain, *themselves*, often come to watch the Dance of the Changer and the Three, and even though it is about them they are still excited and moved by it as though it were a tale never even heard before, let alone lived through. Yet let a dancer miss a movement or color or sound by even the slightest nuance, and the Three will correct him. (And, yes, many times the legended Changer himself, Minnearo, he who started the story, has attended these dances - though often he leaves after the re-creation of his suicide dance.)

It's sometimes difficult to tell one given Loarra from all the others, by the way, despite the complex and subtle technologies of Unicentral, which have provided me with sense filters of all sorts, plus frequency simulators, pattern scopes, special gravity inducers, and a minicomp that takes up more than half of my very tight little island of Earth pasted onto the surface of Loarr and which can do more thinking and analyzing in two seconds than I can do in fifty years. During my four years on Loarr, I got to 'know' several of the Loarra, yet even at the end of my stay I was still never sure just whom I was 'talking' with at any time. I could run through about seventeen or eighteen tests, linking the sense filters with the minicomp, and get a definite answer that way. But the Loarra are a bit short of patience, and by the time I'd get done with all that, whoever it was would usually be off bouncing and sparking into the hellish vapors they call air. So usually I just conducted my researches or negotiations or idle queries, whichever they were that day, with whoever would pay attention to my antigrav 'eyes', and I discovered that it didn't matter much just who I was talking with: none of them made any more sense than the others. They were all, as far as I was and am concerned, totally crazy, incomprehensible, stupid, silly, and plain damn no good.

If that sounds like I'm bitter it's because I am. I've got forty-two murdered men to be bitter about. But back to the unfolding of the greatest legend of an ancient and venerable alien race:

When the Oldest had told them what they wanted to know, the Three came alive with popping and flashing and dancing in the air, Pur just as much as the others. It was all that they had hoped for and more; it was the entire answer to their quest and their problem. It would enable them to create, to transcend any negative cycle-climax they could have devised.

After a time the Three came to themselves and remembered the rituals.

'We offer thanks in the name of Minnearo, whose suicide we are avenging,' Fless said gravely, waving his message in respectful deep-blue spirals.

'We thank you in our own names as well,' said Asterrea.

'And we thank you in the name of no one and nothing,' said Pur, 'for that is the greatest thanks conceivable.

But the Oldest merely sat there, pulsing his dull red, and the Three wondered among themselves. At last the Oldest said, 'To accept thanks is to accept responsibility, and in only-today, as I am, there can be none of that because there can be no new act. I am outside time, you know, which is al-

146

most outside life. All this I have told you is something told to you before, many times, and it will be again.'

Nonetheless, the Three went through all the rituals of thanksgiving, performing them with flawless grace and care – color-and-sound demonstrations, dances, offerings of their own energy, and all the rest. And Pur said, 'It is possible to give thanks for a long-past act or even a mindless reflex, and we do so in the highest.'

The Oldest pulsed dull red and did not answer, and after a time the Three took leave of him.

Armed with the knowledge he had given them, they had no trouble penetrating the barrier protecting Rock, the Oldest's personality-home, and in moments were once again alone with themselves in the raging storm that encircled the vortex. For long minutes they hung in midair, whirling and darting in their most tightly linked patterns while the storm whipped them and the vortex pulled them. Then abruptly they broke their patterns and hurled themselves deliberately into the heart of the vortex itself. In a moment they had disappeared.

They seemed to feel neither motion nor lapse of time as they fell into the vortex. It was a change that came without perception or thought – a change from self to unself, from existence to void. They knew only that they had given themselves up to the vortex, that they were suddenly lost in darkness and a sense of surrounding emptiness which had no dimension. They knew without thinking that if they could have sent forth sound there would have been no echo, that a spark or even a bright flare would have brought no reflection from anywhere. For this was the place of the origin of life, and it was empty. It was up to them to fill it, if it was to be filled.

So they used the secret the Oldest had given them, the secret those at the Beginning had discovered by accident and which only one of the Oldest could have remembered. Having set themselves for this before entering the vortex, they played their individual parts automatically – selfless, unconscious, almost random acts such as even nonliving energy can perform. And when all parts had been completed precisely, correctly, and at just the right time and in just the right sequence, the creating took place.

It was a foodbeast. It formed and took shape before them in the void, and grew and glowed its dull, drab glow until it was whole. For a moment it drifted there, then suddenly it was expelled from the vortex, thrown out violently as though from an explosion – away from the nothingness within, away from darkness and silence into the crashing, whipping violence of the storm outside. And with it went the Three, vomited forth with the primitive bit of life they had made.

Outside, in the storm, the Three went automatically into their tightest motion-sequence, whirling and blinking around each other in desperate striving to maintain themselves amid the savagery that roiled around them. And once again they felt the powerful pull of the vortex behind them, gripping them anew now that they were outside, and they knew that the vortex would draw them in again, this time forever, unless they were able to resist it. But they found that they were nearly spent; they had lost more of themselves in the vortex than they had ever imagined possible. They hardly felt alive now, and somehow they had to withstand the crushing powers of both the storm and the vortex, and had to forge such a strongly interlinked motion-pattern that they would be able to make their way out of this place, back to calm and safety.

And there was only one way they could restore themselves enough for that.

Moving almost as one, they converged upon the mindless foodbeast they had just created, and they ate it.

That's not precisely the end of the Dance of the Changer and the Three – it does go on for a while, telling of the honors given the Three when they returned, and of Minnearo's reaction when he completed his change by reappearing around the life-mote left by a dying windbird, and of how all of the Three turned away from their honors and made their next changes almost immediately – but my own attention never quite follows the rest of it. I always get stuck at that one point in the story, that supremely contradictory moment when the Three destroyed what they had made, when they came away with no more than they had brought with them. It doesn't even achieve irony, and yet it is the emotional highpoint of the Dance as far as the Loarra are concerned. In fact, it's the *whole* point of the Dance, as they've told me with brighter sparkings and flashes than they ever use when talking about anything else, and if the Three had been able to come away from there *without* eating their foodbeast, then their achievement would have been duly noted, applauded, giggled at by the newly changed, and forgotten within two life cycles.

And these are the creatures with whom I had to deal and whose rights I was charged to protect. I was ambassador to a planetful of things that would tell me with a straight face that two and two are orange. And, yes, that's why I'm back on Earth now – and why the rest of the expedition, those who are left alive from it, are back here too.

If you could read the fifteen-microtape report I filed with Unicentral (which you can't, by the way: Unicentral always classifies its failures), it wouldn't tell you anything more about the Loarra than I've just told you in the story of the Dance. In fact, it might tell you less, because although the report contained masses of hard data on the Loarra, plus every theory I could come up with or coax out of the minicomp, it didn't have much about the Dance. And it's only in things like that, attitude-data rather than I.Q. indices, psych reports, and so on, that you can really get the full impact of what we were dealing with on Loarr.

After we'd been on the planet for four Standard Years, after we'd established contact and exchanged gifts and favors and information with the Loarra, after we'd set up our entire mining operation and had it running without hindrance for over three years – after all that, the raid came. One day a sheet of dull purple light swept in from the horizon, and as it got closer I could see that it was a whole colony of the Loarra, their individual colors and fluctuations blending into that single purple mass. I was in the mountain, not outside with the mining extensors, so I saw all of it, and I lived through it.

They flashed in over us like locusts descending, and they hit the crawlers and dredges first. The metal glowed red, then white, then it melted. Then it was just gas that formed billowing clouds rising to the sky. Somewhere inside those clouds was what was left of the elements which had comprised seventeen human beings, who were also vapor now.

I hit the alarm and called everyone in, but only a few made it. The rest were caught in the tunnels when the Loarra swarmed over them, and they went up in smoke too. Then the automatic locks shut, and the mountain was sealed off. And six of us sat there, watching on the screen as the Loarra swept back and forth outside, cleaning up the bits and pieces they'd missed.

I sent out three of my 'eyes', but they too were promptly vaporized.

Then we waited for them to hit the mountain itself . . . half a dozen frightened men huddled in the comp-room, none of us saying anything. Just sweating.

But they didn't come. They swarmed together in a tight spiral, went three times around the mountain, made one final salute-dip and then whirled straight up and out of sight. Only a handful of them were left behind out there.

After a while I sent out a fourth 'eye'. One of the Loarra came over, flitted around it like a firefly, blinked through the spectrum, and settled down to hover in front for talking. It was Pur – a Pur who was a thousand million billion life cycles removed from the Pur we know and love, of course, but nonetheless still pretty much Pur.

I sent out a sequence of lights and movements that translated, roughly, as 'What the hell did you do that for?'

And Pur glowed pale yellow for several seconds, then gave me an answer that doesn't translate. Or, if it does, the translation is just, 'Because.'

Then I asked the question again, in different terms, and she gave me the same answer in different terms. I asked a third time, and a fourth, and she came back with the same thing. She seemed to be enjoying the variations on the dance; maybe she thought we were playing.

Well . . . We'd already sent our distress call by then, so all we could do was wait for a relief ship and hope they wouldn't attack again before the ship came, because we didn't have a chance of fighting them – we were miners, not a military expedition. God knows what any military expedition could have done against energy things, anyway. While we were waiting, I kept sending out the 'eyes', and I kept talking to one Loarra after another. It took three weeks for the ship to get there, and I must have talked to over a hundred of them in that time, and the sum total of what I was told was this:

Their reason for wiping out the mining operation was untranslatable. No, they weren't mad. No, they didn't want us to go away. Yes, we were welcome to the stuff we were taking out of the depths of the Loarran ocean.

And, most importantly: No, they couldn't tell me whether or not they were likely ever to repeat their attack.

So we went away, limped back to Earth, and we all made

our reports to Unicentral. We included, as I said, every bit of data we could think of, including an estimate of the value of the new elements on Loarr – which was something on the order of six times the wealth of Earthsystem. And we put it up to Unicentral as to whether or not we should go back.

Unicentral has been humming and clicking for ten months now, but it hasn't made a decision.

Far Centaurus

A. E. VAN VOGT

*Even the nearest stars are incredibly distant from Earth –
so far away that it takes more than four years for the light
of the closest of them, the Centauri suns, to reach us. Given
the methods of propulsion known to us today, a spaceship
bound for one of those suns would take very much longer
than four years to make the journey – decades, perhaps.
Mankind's first interstellar voyagers must be willing to
spend a lifetime aboard their ship. But, as A. E. van
Vogt, author of such famous science-fiction novels as*
The World of Null-A *and* The Weapon Makers,
*suggests in this classic short story, those pioneering star
voyagers may have a stunning surprise in store for them
when they reach journey's end.*

I wakened with a start, and thought: How was Renfrew
taking it?

I must have moved physically, for blackness edged with
pain closed over me. How long I lay in that agonized faint, I
have no means of knowing. My next awareness was of the
thrusting of the engines that drove the spaceship.

Slowly this time, consciousness returned. I lay very quiet,
feeling the weight of my years of sleep, determined to follow
the routine prescribed so long ago by Pelham.

I didn't want to faint again.

I lay there, and I thought: It was silly to have worried about
Jim Renfrew. He wasn't due to come out of his state of sus-
pended animation for another fifty years.

I began to watch the illuminated face of the clock in the
ceiling. It had registered 23:12; now it was 23:22. The ten
minutes Pelham had suggested for a time lapse between
passivity and initial action was up.

Slowly, I pushed my hand toward the edge of the bed.

Click! My fingers pressed the button that was there. There was a faint hum. The automatic massager began to fumble over my naked form.

First, it rubbed my arms; then it moved to my legs, and so on over my body. As it progressed, I could feel the fine slick of oil that oozed from it working into my dry skin.

A dozen times I could have screamed from the pain of life returning. But in an hour I was able to sit up and turn on the lights.

The small, sparsely furnished, familiar room couldn't hold my attention for more than an instant. I stood up.

The movement must have been too abrupt. I swayed, caught on to the metal column of the bed, and retched discolored stomach juices.

The nausea passed. But it required an effort of will for me to walk to the door, open it, and head along the narrow corridor that led to the control room.

I wasn't supposed to so much as pause there, but a spasm of absolutely dreadful fascination seized me; and I couldn't help it. I leaned over the control chair, and glanced at the chronometer.

It said: 53 years, 7 months, 2 weeks, 0 days, 0 hours and 27 minutes.

Fifty-three years! A little blindly, almost blankly: Back on Earth, the people we had known, the young men we'd gone to college with, that girl who had kissed me at the party given us the night we left – they were all dead. Or dying of old age.

I remembered the girl very vividly. She was pretty, vivacious, a complete stranger. She had laughed as she offered her red lips, and she had said, 'A kiss for the ugly one, too.'

She'd be a grandmother now, or in her grave.

Tears came to my eyes. I brushed them away, and began to heat the can of concentrated liquid that was to be my first food. Slowly, my mind calmed.

Fifty-three years and seven and one half months. I thought drably. Nearly four years over my allotted time. I'd have to do some figuring before I took another dose of Eternity drug. Twenty grains had been calculated to preserve my flesh and my life for exactly fifty years.

The stuff was evidently more potent than Pelham had been able to estimate from his short period advance tests.

I sat tense, narrow-eyed, thinking about that. Abrupt consciousness came of what I was doing. Laughter spat from lips. The sound split the silence like a series of pistol shots, startled me.

But it also relieved me. Was I sitting here actually being critical?

A miss of only four years was bull's-eye across that span of years.

Why, I was alive and still young. Time and space had been conquered. The universe belonged to man.

I ate my 'soup', sipping each spoonful deliberately. I made the bowl last every second of thirty minutes. Then, greatly refreshed, I made my way back to the control room.

This time I paused for a long look through the plates. It took only a few moments to locate Sol, a very brightly glowing star in the approximate center of the rear-view plate.

Alpha Centauri required longer to locate. But it shone finally, a glow point in a light-sprinkled darkness.

I wasted no time trying to estimate their distances. They *looked* right. In fifty-four years we had covered approximately one tenth of the four and one third light-years to the famous nearest star system.

Satisfied, I threaded my way back to the living quarters. Take them in a row, I thought. Pelham first.

As I opened the air-tight door of Pelham's room, a sickening odor of decayed flesh tingled in my nostrils. With a gasp I slammed the door, stood there in the narrow hallway, shuddering.

After a minute, there was still nothing but the reality.

Pelham was dead.

I cannot clearly remember what I did then. I ran; I know that. I flung open Renfrew's door, then Blake's. The clean, sweet smell of their rooms, the sight of their silent bodies on their beds brought back a measure of my sanity.

A great sadness came to me. Poor, brave Pelham. Inventor of the Eternity drug that had made the great plunge into interstellar space possible, he lay dead now from his own invention.

What was it he had said: 'The chances are greatly against any of us dying. But there is what I am calling a death factor of about ten percent, a by-product of the first dose. If our bodies survive the initial shock, they will survive additional doses.'

The death factor must be greater than ten percent. That extra four years the drug had kept me asleep –

Gloomily, I went to the storeroom, and procured my personal spacesuit and a tarpaulin. But even with their help, it was a horrible business. The drug had preserved the body to some extent, but pieces kept falling off as I lifted it.

At last, I carried the tarpaulin and its contents to the air lock, and shoved it into space.

I felt pressed now for time. These waking periods were to be brief affairs, in which what we called the 'current' oxygen was to be used up, but the main reserves were not to be touched. Chemicals in each room slowly refreshed the 'current' air over the years, readying it for the next to awaken.

In some curious defensive fashion, we had neglected to allow for an emergency like the death of one of our members; even as I climbed out of the spacesuit, I could feel the difference in the air I was breathing.

I went first to the radio. It had been calculated that half a light-year was the limit of radio reception, and we were approaching that limit now.

Hurriedly, though carefully, I wrote my report out, then read it into a transcription record, and started sending. I set the record to repeat a hundred times.

In a little more than five months hence, headlines would be flaring on Earth.

I clamped my written report into the ship log book, and added a note for Renfrew at the bottom. It was a brief tribute to Pelham. My praise was heartfelt, but there was another reason behind my note. They had been pals, Renfrew, the engineering genius who built the ship, and Pelham, the great chemist-doctor, whose Eternity drug had made it possible for men to take this fantastic journey into vastness.

It seemed to me that Renfrew, waking up into the great silence of the hurtling ship, would need my tribute to his friend and colleague. It was little enough for me to do, who loved them both.

The note written, I hastily examined the glowing engines, made notations of several instrument readings, and then counted out fifty-five grains of Eternity drug. That was as close as I could get to the amount I felt would be required for one hundred and fifty years.

For a long moment before sleep came, I thought of Renfrew and the terrible shock that was coming to him on top of all the natural reactions to his situations, that would strike deep into his peculiar, sensitive nature –

I stirred uneasily at the picture.

The worry was still in my mind when darkness came.

Almost instantly, I opened my eyes. I lay thinking: The drug! It hadn't worked.

The draggy feel of my body warned me of the truth. I lay very still watching the clock overhead. This time it was easier to follow the routine except that, once more, I could not refrain from examining the chronometer as I passed through the galley.

It read: 201 years, 1 month, 3 weeks, 5 days, 7 hours, 8 minutes.

I sipped my bowl of that super soup, then went eagerly to the big log book.

It is utterly impossible for me to describe the thrill that coursed through me, as I saw the familiar hand-writing of Blake, and then, as I turned back the pages, of Renfrew.

My excitement drained slowly, as I read what Renfrew had written. It was a report; nothing more: gravitometric readings, a careful calculation of the distance covered, a detailed report on the performance of the engines, and, finally, an estimate of our speed variations, based on the seven consistent factors.

It was a splendid mathematical job, a first-rate scientific analysis. But that was all there was. No mention of Pelham, not a word of comment on what I had written or on what had happened.

Renfrew had wakened; and, if his report was any criterion, he might as well have been a robot.

I knew better than that.

So – I saw as I began to read Blake's report – did Blake.

Bill:
TEAR THIS SHEET OUT WHEN YOU'VE READ IT!

Well, the worst has happened. We couldn't have asked fate to give us an unkindlier kick in the pants. I hate to think of Pelham being dead – what a man he was, what a friend – but we all knew the risk we were taking, he more than any of us. Space rest his great soul.

But Renfrew's case is now serious. After all, we were worried, wondering how he'd take his first awakening, let alone a bang between the eyes like Pelham's death. And I think that first anxiety was justified.

As you and I have always known, Renfrew was one of Earth's fair-haired boys. Just imagine any one human being born with his combination of looks, money, and intelligence. His great fault was that he never let the future trouble him. With that dazzling personality of his, and the crew of worshipping women and yes-men around him, he didn't have much time for any thing but the present.

Realities always struck him like a thunderbolt. He could leave those three ex-wives of his – and they weren't so ex, if you ask me – without grasping that it was forever.

That good-bye party was enough to put anyone into a sort of mental haze when it came to realities. To wake up a hundred years later, and realize that those he loved had withered, died, and been eaten by worms – we-e-ll!

(I put it baldly like that because the human mind always thinks the worst angles, no matter how it censors speech.)

I personally counted on Pelham acting as a sort of psychological support to Renfrew; and we both know that Pelham recognized the extent of his influence over Renfrew. That influence must be replaced. Try to think of something, Bill, while you're charging around doing the routine work. We've got to live with that guy after we all wake up at the end of the five hundred years.

Tear out this sheet. What follows is routine.

NED

I burned the letter in the incinerator, examined the two sleeping bodies – how deathly quiet they lay! – and then returned to the control room.

In the plate, the sun was a very bright star, a jewel set in black velvet, a gorgeous, shining brilliant.

Alpha Centauri was brighter. It was a radiant light in that panoply of black and glitter. It was still impossible to make out the separate suns of Alpha A, B, C, and Proxima, but their combined light brought a sense of awe and majesty.

Excitement blazed inside me; and consciousness came of the glory of this trip we were making, the first men to head for far Centaurus, the first men to dare aspire to the stars.

Even the thought of Earth failed to dim that surging tide of wonder; the thought that seven, possibly eight generations, had been born since our departure; the thought that the girl who had given me the sweet remembrance of her red lips was now known to her descendants as their great-great-great-great-grandmother – if she was remembered at all.

The immense time involved, the whole idea, was too meaningless for emotion.

I did my work, took my third dose of the drug, and went to bed. The sleep found me still without a plan about Renfrew.

When I woke up, alarm bells were ringing.

I lay still. There was nothing else to do. If I had moved, consciousness would have slid from me. Though it was mental torture even to think it, I realized that, no matter what the danger, the quickest way was to follow my routine to the second and in every detail.

Somehow I did it. The bells clanged and *brrred*, but I lay there until it was time to get up. The clamor was hideous, as I passed through the control room. But I *passed* through, and sat for half an hour sipping my soup.

The conviction came to me that if that sound continued much longer, Blake and Renfrew would surely waken from their sleep.

At last, I felt free to cope with the emergency. Breathing hard, I eased myself into the control chair, cut off the mind-wrecking alarms, and switched on the plates.

A fire glowed at me from the rear-view plate. It was a colossal *white* fire, longer than it was wide, and filling nearly a quarter of the whole sky. The hideous thought came to me that we must be within a few million miles of some monstrous sun that had recently roared into this part of space.

Frantically, I manipulated the distance estimators – and then for a moment stared in blank disbelief at the answers that clicked metallically onto the product plate.

Seven miles! *Only* seven miles! Curious is the human mind. A moment before, when I had thought of it as an abnormally shaped sun, it hadn't resembled anything but an incandescent mass. Abruptly, now, I saw that it had a solid outline, an unmistakable material shape.

Stunned, I leaped to my feet because –

It was a spaceship! An enormous, mile-long ship. Rather – I sank back into my seat, subdued by the catastrophe I was witnessing, and consciously adjusting my mind – the flaming hell of what had been a spaceship. Nothing that had been alive could possibly still be conscious in that horror of ravenous fire. The only possibility was that the crew had succeeded in launching lifeboats.

Like a madman, I searched the heavens for a light, a glint of metal that would show the presence of survivors.

There was nothing but the night and the stars and the hell of burning ship.

After a long time, I noticed that it was farther away, and seemed to be receding. Whatever drive forces had matched its velocity to ours must be yielding to the fury of the energies that were consuming the ship.

I began to take pictures, and I felt justified in turning on the oxygen reserves. As it withdrew into distance, the miniature nova that had been a torpedo-shaped space liner began to change color, to lose its white intensity. It became a red fire silhouetted against darkness. My last glimpse showed it as a long, dull glow that looked like nothing else than a cherry-colored nebula seen edge on, like a glaze reflecting from the night beyond a far horizon.

I had already, in between observations, done everything else required of me; and now, I reconnected the alarm system, and, very reluctantly, my mind seething with speculation, returned to bed.

As I lay waiting for my final dosage of the trip to take effect, I thought: the great star system of Alpha Centauri must have inhabited planets. If my calculations were correct, we were only one point six light-years from the main Alpha group of suns, slightly nearer than that to red Proxima.

Here was proof that the universe had at least one other supremely intelligent race. Wonders beyond our wildest expectations were in store for us. Thrill on thrill of anticipation raced through me.

It was only at the last instant, as sleep was already grasping at my brain that the realization struck that I had completely forgotten about the problem of Renfrew.

I felt no alarm. Surely, even Renfrew would come alive in that great fashion of his when confronted by a complex alien civilization.

Our troubles were over.

Excitement must have bridged that final one hundred fifty years of time. Because, when I wakened, I thought:

'We're here! It's over, the long night, the incredible

journey. We'll all be waking, seeing each other, as well as the civilization out there. Seeing, too, the great Centauri suns.'

The strange thing, it struck me as I lay there exulting, was that the time seemed long. And yet . . . yet I had been awake only three times, and only once for the equivalent of a full day.

In the truest sense of meaning, I had seen Blake and Renfrew – and Pelham – no more than a day and a half ago. I had had only thirty-six hours of consciousness since a pair of soft lips had set themselves against mine, and clung in the sweetest kiss of my life.

Then why this feeling that millenniums had ticked by, second on slow second? Why this eerie, empty awareness of a journey through fathomless, unending night?

Was the human mind so easily fooled?

It seemed to me, finally, that the answer was that *I* had been alive for those five hundred years, all my cells and my organs had existed, and it was not even impossible that some part of my brain had been horrendously aware throughout the entire unthinkable period.

And there was, of course, the additional psychological fact that I knew now that five hundred years had gone by, and that –

I saw with a mental start, that my ten minutes were up. Cautiously, I turned on the massager.

The gentle, padded hands had been working on me for about fifteen minutes when my door opened; the light clicked on, and there stood Blake.

The too-sharp movement of turning my head to look at him made me dizzy. I closed my eyes, and heard him walk across the room toward me.

After a minute, I was able to look at him again without seeing blurs. I saw then that he was carrying a bowl of the soup. He stood staring down at me with a strangely grim expression on his face.

At last, his long, thin countenance relaxed into a wan grin. ' 'Lo, Bill,' he said. '*Ssshh!*' he hissed immediately. 'Now, don't try to speak. I'm going to start feeding you this soup while you're still lying down. The sooner you're up, the better I'll like it.'

He was grim again, as he finished almost as if it was an afterthought: 'I've been up for two weeks.'

He sat down on the edge of the bed, and ladled out a spoonful of 'soup'. There was silence, then, except for the rustling sound of the massager. Slowly, the strength flowed through my body; and with each passing second, I became more aware of the grimness of Blake.

'What about Renfrew?' I managed finally, hoarsely. 'He awake?'

Blake hesitated, then nodded. His expression darkened with frown; he said simply:

'He's mad, Bill, stark, staring mad. I had to tie him up. I've got him now in his room. He's quieter now, but at the beginning he was a gibbering maniac.'

'Are you crazy?' I whispered at last. 'Renfrew was never so sensitive as that. Depressed and sick, yes; but the mere passage of time, abrupt awareness that all his friends are dead, couldn't make him insane.'

Blake was shaking his head. 'It isn't only that. Bill – '

He paused, then: 'Bill, I want you to prepare your mind for the greatest shock it's ever had.'

I stared up at him with an empty feeling inside me. 'What do you mean?'

He went on, grimacing: 'I know you'll be able to take it. So don't get scared. You and I, Bill, are just a couple of lugs. We're along because we went to U with Renfrew and Pelham. Basically, it wouldn't matter to insensitives like us whether we landed in 1,000,000 B.C. or A.D. We'd just look around and say: "Fancy seeing you here, mug!" or "Who was that pterodactyl I saw you with last night?" "That wasn't no pterodactyl; that was Unthahorsten's bulbous-brained wife."'

'For Mars' sake,' I whispered, 'get to the point. What's up?'

Blake rose to his feet. 'Bill, after I'd read your reports about, and seen the photographs of, that burning ship, I got an idea. The Alpha suns were pretty close two weeks ago, only about six months away at our average speed of five hundred miles a second. I thought to myself: "I'll see if I can tune in some of their radio stations".

'Well,' he smiled wryly, 'I got hundreds in a few minutes. They came in all over the seven wave dials, with bell-like clarity.'

He paused; he stared down at me, and his smile was a sickly thing. 'Bill,' he groaned, 'we're the prize fools in creation. When I told Renfrew the truth, he folded up like ice melting into water.'

Once more, he paused; the silence was too much for my straining nerves.

'For Heaven's sake, man – ' I began. And stopped. And lay there, very still. Just like that the lightning of understanding flashed on me. My blood seemed to thunder through my veins. At last, weakly, I said: 'You mean – '

Blake nodded. 'Yeah,' he said. 'That's the way it is. And they've already spotted us with their spy rays and energy screens. A ship's coming out to meet us.

'I only hope,' he finished gloomily, 'they can do something for Jim.'

I was sitting in the control chair an hour later when I saw the glint in the darkness. There was a flash of bright silver, that exploded into size. The next instant, an enormous spaceship had matched our velocity less than a mile away.

Blake and I looked at each other. 'Did they say,' I said shakily, 'that that ship left its hangar ten minutes ago?'

Blake nodded. 'They can make the trip from Earth to Centauri in three hours,' he said.

I hadn't heard that before. Something happened inside my brain. 'What!' I shouted. 'Why, it's taken us five hund – '

I stopped; I sat there. 'Three hours!' I whispered. 'How *could* we have forgotten human progress?'

In the silence that fell then, we watched a dark hole open in the clifflike wall that faced us. Into this cavern, I directed our ship.

The rear-view plate showed that the cave entrance was closing. Ahead of us lights flashed on, and focused on a door. As I eased our craft to the metal floor, a face flickered onto our radio plate.

'Cassellahat!' Blake whispered in my ear. 'The only chap who's talked direct to me so far.'

It was a distinguished, a scholarly looking head and face that peered at us. Cassellahat smiled, and said:

'You may leave your ship, and go through the door you see.'

I had a sense of empty spaces around us, as we climbed gingerly out into the vast receptor chamber. Interplanetary spaceship hangars were like that, I reminded myself. Only this one had an alien quality that –

'Nerves!' I thought sharply.

But I could see that Blake felt it, too. A silent duo, we filed through the doorway into a hallway that opened into a very large, luxurious room.

It was such a room as a king or a movie actress on set might have walked into without blinking. It was all hung with gorgeous tapestries – that is, for a moment, I thought they were tapestries; then I saw they weren't. They were – I couldn't decide.

I had seen expensive furniture in some of the apartments Renfrew maintained. But these chesterfields, chairs and tables glittered at us, as if they were made of a matching design of differently colored fires. No, that was wrong; they didn't glitter at all. They –

Once more I couldn't decide.

I had no time for more detailed examination. For a man arrayed very much as we were was rising from one of the chairs. I recognized Cassellahat.

He came forward, smiling. Then he slowed, his nose wrinkling. A moment later, he hastily shook our hands, then swiftly retreated to a chair ten feet away, and sat down rather primly.

It was an astoundingly ungracious performance. But I was glad that he had drawn back that way. Because, as he shook my hand so briefly, I had caught a faint whiff of perfume from him. It was a vaguely unpleasant odor; and, besides – a man using perfume in quantities!

I shuddered. What kind of foppish nonsense had the human race gone in for?

He was motioning us to sit down. I did so, wondering: Was this our reception? The erstwhile radio operator began:

'About your friend, I must caution you. He is a schizoid type, and our psychologists will be able to effect a temporary recovery only for the moment. A permanent cure will require a longer period, and your fullest cooperation. Fall in readily with all Mr Renfrew's plans, unless, of course, he takes a dangerous turn.

'But now' – he squirted us a smile – 'permit me to welcome you to the four planets of Centauri. It is a great moment for me, personally. From my childhood, I have been trained for the sole purpose of being your mentor and guide; and naturally I am overjoyed that the time has come when my exhaustive studies of the middle period American language and customs can be put to the practical use for which they were intended.'

He didn't look overjoyed. He was wrinkling his nose in that funny way I had already noticed, and there was a generally pained expression on his face. But it was his words that shocked me.

'What do you mean,' I asked, 'studies in American? Don't people speak the universal language any more?'

'Of course' – he smiled – 'but the language has developed to a point where – I might as well be frank – you would have difficulty understanding such a simple word as "yeih".'

'Yeih?' Blake echoed.

'Meaning "yes".'

'Oh!'

We sat silent, Blake chewing his lower lip. It was Blake who finally said:

'What kind of places are the Centauri planets? You said something on the radio about the population centers having reverted to the city structure again.'

'I shall be happy,' said Cassellahat, 'to show you as many of our great cities as you care to see. You are our guests, and several million credits have been placed at your separate accounts for you to use as you see fit.'

'Gee!' said Blake.

'I must, however,' Cassellahat went on, 'give you a warning. It is important that you do not disillusion our peoples about yourselves. Therefore, you must never wander around the streets, or mingle with the crowds in any way. Always, your contact should be via newsreels, radio, or from the *inside* of a closed machine. If you have any plan to marry, you must now finally give up the idea.'

'I don't get it!' Blake said wonderingly; and he spoke for us both.

Cassellahat finished firmly: 'It is important that no one becomes aware that you have an offensive physical odor. It might damage your financial prospects considerably.

'And now' – he stood up – 'for the time being, I shall leave you. I hope you don't mind if I wear a mask in the future in your presence. I wish you well, gentlemen, and –'

He paused, glanced past us, said: 'Ah, here is your friend.'

I whirled, and I could see Blake twisting, staring –

'Hi, there, fellows,' Renfrew said cheerfully from the door, then wryly: 'Have we ever been a bunch of suckers!'

I felt choked. I raced up to him, caught his hand, hugged him. Blake was trying to do the same.

When we finally released Renfrew, and looked around, Cassellahat was gone.

Which was just as well. I had been wanting to punch him in the nose for his final remarks.

'Well, here goes!' Renfrew said.

He looked at Blake and me, grinned, rubbed his hands together gleefully, and added:

'For a week I've been watching, thinking up questions to ask this cluck and – '

He faced Cassellahat. 'What,' he began, 'makes the speed of light constant?'

Cassellahat did not even blink. 'Velocity equals the cube of the cube root of gd,' he said, 'd being the depth of the space-time continuum, g the total toleration or gravity, as you would say, of all the matter in that continuum.'

'How are planets formed?'

'A sun must balance itself in the space that it is in. It throws out matter as a sea vessel does anchors. That's a very rough description. I could give it to you in mathematical formula, but I'd have to write it down. After all, I'm not a scientist. These are merely facts that I've known from childhood, or so it seems.'

'Just a minute,' said Renfrew, puzzled. 'A sun throws this matter out without any pressure other than its – desire – to balance itself?'

Cassellahat stared at him. 'Of course not. The reason, the pressure involved, is very potent, I assure you. Without such a balance, the sun would fall out of this space. Only a few bachelor suns have learned how to maintain stability without planets.'

'A few what?' echoed Renfrew.

I could see that he had been jarred into forgetting the questions he had been intending to ask one by swift one. Cassellahat's words cut across my thought; he said:

'A bachelor sun is a very old, cooled class M star. The hottest one known has a temperature of one hundred ninety degrees Fahrenheit, the coldest forty-eight. Literally, a bachelor is a rogue, crochety with age. Its main feature is that it permits no matter, no planets, not even gases in its vicinity.'

Renfrew sat silent, frowning, thoughtful. I seized the opportunity to carry on a train of idea.

'This business,' I said, 'of knowing all this stuff without being a scientist, interests me. For instance, back home every kid understood the atomic-rocket principle practically from the day he was born. Boys of eight and ten rode around in specially made toys, took them apart and put them together again. They *thought* rocket-atomic, and any new development in the field was just pie for them to absorb.

'Now, here's what I'd like to know: what is the parallel here to that particular angle?'

'The adeledicnander force,' said Cassellahat. 'I've already tried to explain it to Mr Renfrew, but his mind seems to balk at some of the most simple aspects.'

Renfrew roused himself, grimaced. 'He's been trying to tell me that electrons think; and I won't swallow it.'

Cassellahat shook his head. 'Not think; they don't think. But they have a psychology.'

'Electronic psychology!' I said.

'Simply adeledicnander,' Cassellahat replied. 'Any child – '

Renfrew groaned: 'I know. Any child of six could tell me.'

He turned to us. 'That's why I lined up a lot of questions. I figured that if we got a good intermediate grounding, we might be able to slip into this adeledicnander stuff the way their kids do.'

He faced Cassellahat. 'Next question,' he said. 'What – '

Cassellahat had been looking at his watch. 'I'm afraid, Mr Renfrew,' he interrupted, 'that if you and I are going to be on the ferry to the Pelham planet, we'd better leave now. You can ask your questions on the way.'

'What's all this?' I chimed in.

Renfrew explained: 'He's taking me to the great engineering laboratories in the European mountains of Pelham. Want to come along?'

'Not me,' I said.

Blake shrugged. 'I don't fancy getting into one of those suits Cassellahat has provided for us, designed to keep our odor in, but not theirs out.'

He finished: 'Bill and I will stay here and play poker for some of that five million credits' worth of dough we've got in the State bank.'

Cassellahat turned at the door; there was a distinct frown on

166

the flesh mask he wore. 'You treat our government's gift very
lightly.'

'Yeih!' said Blake.

'So we stink,' said Blake.

It was nine days since Cassellahat had taken Renfrew to the
planet Pelham; and our only contact had been a radio tele-
phone call from Renfrew on the third day, telling us not to
worry.

Blake was standing at the window of our penthouse apartment in the city Newmerica; and I was on my back on a couch,
in my mind a mixture of thoughts involving Renfrew's
potential insanity and all the things I had heard and seen about
the history of the past five hundred years.

I roused myself. 'Quit it,' I said. 'We're faced with a
change in the metabolism of the human body, probably due to
the many different foods from remote stars that they eat. They
must be able to smell better, too, because just being near us is
agony to Cassellahat, whereas we only notice an unpleasant-
ness from him. It's a case of three of us against billions of them.
Frankly, I don't see an early victory over the problem, so let's
just take it quietly.'

There was no answer; so I returned to my reverie. My first
radio message to Earth had been picked up; and so, when the
interstellar drive was invented in A.D. 2320, less than one
hundred forty years after our departure, it was realized what
would eventually happen.

In our honor, the four habitable planets of the Alpha A and
B suns were called Renfrew, Pelham, Blake and Endicott.
Since 2320, the populations of the four planets had become so
dense that a total of nineteen billion people now dwelt on their
narrowing land spaces. This in spite of migrations to the
planets of more distant stars.

The space liner I had seen burning in A.D. 2511 was the only
ship ever lost on the Earth-Centauri lane. Traveling at full
speed, its screens must have reacted against our spaceship.
All the automatics would instantly have flashed on; and as
those defenses were not able at that time to stop a ship that had
gone Minus Infinity, every recoil engine aboard had probably
blown up.

Such a thing could not happen again. So enormous had been
the progress in the adeledicnander field of power, that the

greatest liners could stop dead in the full fury of midflight.

We had been told not to feel any sense of blame for that one disaster, as many of the most important advances in adeledicnander electronic psychology had been made as the result of theoretical analyses of that great catastrophe.

I grew aware that Blake had flung himself disgustedly into a nearby chair.

'Boy, oh, boy,' he said, 'this is going to be some life for us. We can all anticipate about fifty more years of being pariahs in a civilization where we can't even understand how the simplest machines work.'

I stirred uneasily. I had had similar thoughts. But I said nothing. Blake went on:

'I must admit, after I first discovered the Centauri planets had been colonized, I had pictures of myself bowling over some dame, and marrying her.'

Involuntarily, my mind leaped to the memory of a pair of lips lifting up to mine. I shook myself. I said:

'I wonder how Renfrew is taking all this. He – '

A familiar voice from the door cut off my words. 'Renfrew,' it said, 'is taking things beautifully now that the first shock has yielded to resignation, and resignation to purpose.'

We had turned to face him by the time he finished. Renfrew walked slowly towards us, grinning. Watching him, I felt uncertain as to just how to take his built-up sanity.

He was at his best. His dark, wavy hair was perfectly combed. His startlingly blue eyes made his whole face come alive. He was a natural physical wonder; and at his normal he had all the shine and swagger of an actor in a carefully tailored picture.

He wore that shine and swagger now. He said:

'I've bought a spaceship, fellows. Took all my money and part of yours, too. But I knew you'd back me up. Am I right?'

'Why, sure,' Blake and I echoed.

Blake went on alone: 'What's the idea?'

'I get it,' I chimed in. 'We'll cruise all over the universe, live our life span exploring new worlds. Jim, you've got something there. Blake and I were just going to enter a suicide pact.'

Renfrew was smiling. 'We'll cruise for a while anyway.'

Two days later, Cassellahat having offered no objection and no advice about Renfrew, we were in space.

It was a curious three months that followed. For a while I felt a sense of awe at the vastness of the cosmos. Silent planets swung into our viewing plates, and faded into remoteness behind us, leaving nostalgic memory of uninhabited, wind-lashed forests and plains, deserted, swollen seas and nameless suns.

The sight and the remembrance brought loneliness like an ache, and the knowledge, the slow knowledge, that this journeying was not lifting the weight of strangeness that had settled upon us ever since our arrival at Alpha Centauri.

There was nothing here for our souls to feed on, nothing that would satisfactorily fill one year of our life, let alone fifty. Nothing, nothing.

I watched the realization grow on Blake, and I waited for a sign from Renfrew that he felt it, too. The sign didn't come. That of itself worried me; then I grew aware of something else. Renfrew was watching us. Watching us with a hint in his manner of secret knowledge, a suggestion of secret purpose.

My alarm grew; and Renfrew's perpetual cheerfulness didn't help any. I was lying on my bunk at the end of the third month, thinking uneasily about the whole unsatisfactory situation, when my door opened, and Renfrew came in.

He carried a paralyzer gun and a rope. He pointed the gun at me, and said.

'Sorry, Bill. Cassellahat told me to take no chances, so just lie quiet while I tie you up.'

'Blake!' I bellowed.

Renfrew shook his head gently. 'No use,' he said. 'I was in his room first.'

The gun was steady in his fingers, his blue eyes were steely. All I could do was tense my muscles against the ropes as he tied me, and trust to the fact that I was twice as strong, at least, as he was.

I thought in dismay: Surely I could prevent him from tying me too tightly.

He stepped back finally, and said again, 'Sorry, Bill.' He added: 'I hate to tell you this, but both of you went off the deep end mentally when we arrived at Centauri; and this is the cure prescribed by the psychologists whom Cassellahat consulted. You're supposed to get a shock as big as the one that knocked you for a loop.'

The first time I'd paid no attention to his mention of Cassellahat's name. Now my mind flared with understanding.

Incredibly, Renfrew had been told that Blake and I were mad. All these months he had been held steady by a sense of responsibility toward us. It was a beautiful psychological scheme. The only thing was: *what* shock was going to be administered?

Renfrew's voice cut off my thought. He said:

'It won't be long now. We're already entering the field of the bachelor sun.'

'Bachelor sun!' I yelled.

He made no reply. The instant the door closed behind him, I began to work on my bonds; all the time I was thinking:

What was it Cassellahat had said? Bachelor suns maintained themselves in this space by a precarious balancing.

In *this* space! The sweat poured down my face, as I pictured ourselves being precipitated into another plane of the space-time continuum – I could feel the ship falling when I finally worked my hands free of the rope.

I hadn't been tied long enough for the cords to interfere with my circulation. I headed for Blake's room. In two minutes we were on our way to the control cabin.

Renfrew didn't see us till we had him. Blake grabbed his gun; I hauled him out of the control chair with one mighty heave, and dumped him onto the floor.

He lay there, unresisting, grinning up at us. 'Too late,' he taunted. 'We're approaching the first point of intolerance, and there's nothing you can do except prepare for the shock.'

I scarcely heard him. I plumped myself into the chair, and glared into the viewing plates. Nothing showed. That stumped me for a second. Then I saw the recorder instruments. They were trembling furiously, registering a body of INFINITE size.

For one long moment I stared crazily at those incredible figures. Then plunged the decelerator far over. Before that pressure of full-driven adeledicnander, the machine grew rigid; I had a sudden fantastic picture of two irresistible forces in full collision. Gasping, I jerked the power out of gear.

We were still falling.

'An orbit,' Blake was saying. 'Get us into an orbit.'

With shaking fingers, I pounded one out on the keyboard, basing my figures on a sun of Sol-ish size, gravity, and mass.

The bachelor wouldn't let us have it.

I tried another orbit, and a third, and more – finally one that would have given us an orbit around mighty Antares itself. But the deadly reality remained. The ship plunged on, down and down.

And there was nothing visible on the plates, not a real shadow of substance. It seemed to me once that I could make out a vague blur of greater darkness against the black reaches of space. But the stars were few in every direction and it was impossible to be sure.

Finally, in despair, I whirled out of the seat, and knelt beside Renfrew, who was still making no effort to get up.

'Listen, Jim,' I pleaded, 'what did you do this for? What's going to happen?'

He was smiling easily. 'Think,' he said, 'of an old, crusty, human bachelor. He maintains a relationship with his fellows, but the association is as remote as that which exists between a bachelor sun and the stars in the galaxy of which it is a part.'

He added: 'Any second now we'll strike the first period of intolerance. It works in jumps like quantum, each period being four hundred ninety-eight years, seven months and eight days plus a few hours.'

It sounded like gibberish. 'But what's going to happen?' I urged. 'For Heaven's sake, man!'

He gazed up at me blandly; and, looking at him, I had the sudden, wondering realization that he was sane, the old, completely rational Jim Renfrew, made better somehow, stronger. He said quietly:

'Why, it'll just knock us out of its toleration area; and in doing so will put us back – '

JERK!

The lurch was immensely violent. With a bang, I struck the floor, skidded, and then a hand – Renfrew's – caught me. And it was all over.

I stood up, conscious that we were no longer falling. I looked at the instrument board. All the lights were dim, untroubled, the needles firmly at zero. I turned and stared at Renfrew, and at Blake, who was ruefully picking himself up from the floor.

Renfrew said persuasively: 'Let me at the control board, Bill. I want to set our course for Earth.'

For a long minute, I gazed at him; and then, slowly, I stepped aside. I stood by as he set the controls and pulled the accelerator over. Renfrew looked up.

'We'll reach Earth in about eight hours,' he said, 'and it'll be a year and a half after we left five hundred years ago.'

Something began to tug at the roof of my cranium. It took several seconds before I realized that it was my brain jumping with the tremendous understanding that suddenly flowed in upon me.

The bachelor sun, I thought dazedly. In easing us out of its field of toleration, it had simply precipitated us into a period of time beyond its field. Renfrew had said . . . had said that it worked in jumps of . . . four hundred ninety-eight and some seven months and –

But what about the ship? Wouldn't twenty-seventh century adeledicnander brought to the twenty-second century, before it was invented, change the course of history? I mumbled the question.

Renfrew shook his head. 'Do *we* understand it? Do we even dare monkey with the raw power inside those engines? I'll say not. As for the ship, we'll keep it for our own private use.'

'B-but – ' I began.

He cut me off. 'Look, Bill,' he said, 'here's the situation: that girl who kissed you – don't think I didn't see you falling like a ton of bricks – is going to be sitting beside you fifty years from now, when *your* voice from space reports to Earth that you had wakened on your first lap of the first trip to Centaurus.'

That's exactly what happened.

THE END

THIS IS THE WAY THE WORLD BEGINS by J. T. McINTOSH

From the holiday planet of Paradiso one could go on many exciting tours and excursions – Mars, Venus, the Moon, even the most distant and alien worlds were accessible to the inquisitive holidaymaker, courtesy of Starways Inc. – the giant combine which owned Paradiso and over half the galaxy.

But of all Starways illustrious trips, there was really only one which interested Ram Burrell – the one which Starways seemed to actually discourage people from taking ... the trip to planet Earth.

0 552 10432 9 – 70p

WILL-O-THE-WISP by THOMAS BURNETT SWANN

Will-o-the-wisp – the light that danced across the Devon moors – enticing the good puritan people to death and devilment ... For up on the tors dwelt the infamous Gubbings who crucified their victims, murdered and bewitched ...

Were they really warlocks, or were they creatures of fantasy from another time, another planet?

Robert Herrick, poet, vicar and pagan, the golden giant with a lusty heart, dared to brave the moors and challenge the ancient myth ...

0 552 10358 6 – 60p

THE SHAPE OF THINGS TO COME by H. G. WELLS

First published in 1933 it was described by Wells as 'A Short History of the Future', and spans the period from A.D. 1929 to the end of the year 2105. It is a chronicle of world events, a memorable catalogue of prediction involving war, technical revolution and the cultural changes which await mankind in the years to come . . .

0 552 09532 X – 95p

THE SHAPE OF FURTHER THINGS by BRIAN ALDISS

'Haven't you ever thought to yourself after a pleasant evening – or even a dull afternoon – that if you could but have it all again, preferably in slow motion, then you could trace in it all the varied strands of your life?'

In this provocative book Brian Aldiss seeks to recapture some of the strands of his life, and in basic diary form he works alternately back into the past and forward into the future; the realities of our world alternate with the unrealities of fantasy.

The result is an autobiography spanning one month – a month in the life of a speculative writer, with topics ranging from the growth of science fiction in Britain today to new theories on the nature and importance of dreams.

0 552 09533 8 – 65p

THE SHIP WHO SANG by ANNE McCAFFREY

The brain was perfect, the tiny, crippled body useless. So technology rescued the brain and put it in an environment that conditioned it to live in a different kind of body – a spaceship. Here the human mind, more subtle, infinitely more complex than any computer ever devised, could be linked to the massive and delicate strengths, the total recall, and the incredible speeds of space. But the brain behind the ship was entirely feminine – complex, loving, strong, weak, gentle, savage – a personality, all-woman, called Helva. . . .

0 552 10163 X – 80p

RESTOREE by ANNE McCAFFREY

There was a sudden stench of a dead sea creature . . .

There was the horror of a huge black shape closing over her . . .

There was nothing . . .

Then there were pieces of memory . . . isolated fragments that were so horrible her mind refused to accept them . . . intense heat and shivering cold . . . excruciating pain . . . dismembered pieces of the human body . . . sawn bones and searing screams . . .

And when she awoke she found she was in a world that was not earth, and with a face and body that were not her face and body.

She had become a Restoree. . . .

0 552 10161 3 – 75p

A SELECTED LIST OF CORGI BOOKS
FOR YOUR READING PLEASURE